# Disclaimer

This is a work of fiction. Names, characters, businesses, places, events and incidents are either products of the author's imagination or used in a fictitious manner. Although it is based around the famous ground there is no official association with the Marylebone Cricket Club (MCC) or Lord's Cricket Ground. Similarly The Cricket Club of India, The Bombay Yacht Club and Brabourne Stadium.

The Indian Mouse Cricket Caper
By Mark Trenowden

ISBN - 978-1-5272-0356-3

© 2016 Mark Trenowden. All rights reserved


Dotball Books
Halifax
NS Canada

www.marktrenowden.com

# The Indian Mouse Cricket Caper

Mark Trenowden

For Uncle Michael

BY THE SAME AUTHOR

The Mystery of the Goodfellowes' Code

The Miracle of Bean's Bullion

The Mouse Cricket Caper

## Chapter One

*There's always one,* Neville Knox thought to himself as his tour group fanned out in front of him. There had been one in that morning's group, and despite the fact that presumably they'd all just had lunch, here was another. It wasn't as if he'd spelt it out in some sort of complicated code.

'Would you be so kind as to refrain from eating whilst on the tour?' It wasn't a lot to ask, was it?

The mild-mannered and expectant gathering had murmured their acceptance of the request. But, now barely twenty-five minutes in, there was someone flouting the regulation. Okay, regulation was perhaps a bit strong. One teeny-weeny little rule was all he'd asked of them. Perhaps it did seem a little bit pernickety, but food tended to mean litter, and it was November after all. Yes, November, not a month that one instantly associates with cricket. With the cricket season over, the ground's workforce had more pressing projects than litter collecting on their hands. However, London as a tourist destination has a year-round appeal, and for those visitors interested in cricket, Lord's Cricket Ground is pretty high on their 'to-do' list. So the tours of the ground carried on throughout the winter months, and as long as they did so, Neville would continue to make his request.

'So we are now standing bang smack in the middle of the ground. On our right, the iconic pavilion built in 1889, and to our left, the Media Centre, completed 110 years later,' Neville described the panoramic view.

Buster Bosch nodded knowingly to himself. Visiting from Johannesburg, he'd been looking forward to his visit and had read several books on the subject. His son Titus, who'd been dragged along for the advancement of his cricketing knowledge, was finding it difficult to work up the same level of interest. Instead, he was practicing the ancient schoolboy art of concealed eating. Despite his expertise, perfected in the back row of the school classroom back in Jo'burg, he was having trouble. Prising the finger off a wrapped KitKat chocolate bar with one hand in the pocket of an anorak was proving difficult. There was nothing else for it. Edging behind a lady in a flowery raincoat, he furtively removed the chocolate and slid the bar from its wrapper. He ran a nail the length of the foil and parted a chocolate finger from the others.

'We're standing in the new grandstand completed in 1998...' Neville explained, keeping to his script whilst pinpointing the breaker of his rules with unerring accuracy. 'The third such building, replacing the previous structure, which was completed in 1925.'

Titus licked his lips and, with a snap, broke off the first finger. A nanosecond after the 'snap', Neville snapped too.

'I said, NO eating!' he boomed.

For an instant, Titus pulled a face reminiscent of the famous painting 'The Scream', throwing his hands in the air and the chocolate finger over his shoulder in the process. Neville returned to his script without missing a beat. His outburst had had the desired effect, and he resumed the tour as if nothing had happened.

The chocolate finger left the scene of the crime, flying end over into the vacant seating behind the little group.

Gatt, who'd been keeping his distance but monitoring the progress of the visitors, followed its flight path. As the self-appointed gastronome of the Lord's mouse colony, he more than any of the others suffered in the off-season. He thought about the rather samey meals of the last week or two. In this period, the mice had managed to gather enough to live on from the pavilion kitchen, which was still catering for functions. They had to be careful though, taking small quantities of what there seemed to be a lot of, so as not to draw attention. In the main, that meant boring things like rice and flour and that brittle stuff that hurt your teeth and really didn't taste too good anyway. *Pasta*, that's what they called it, the mice couldn't see what people saw in it. There certainly was a lot of that, in lots of different shapes and sizes, but sadly not different flavours. They all missed the little treats that came with match days, and more exactly the paying public. What an interesting selection they brought with them and how careless they were with it.

But this was where vigilance paid off. If you were patient enough, there were still opportunities to pick up some of the more delicious things in life. Just the other day, he'd relieved a decorator of half a sausage roll he'd put down for just a moment. Gatt remembered it with a smile. He'd scoffed the lot, which had made him feel a little peculiar. *That was very greedy, Gatt*, he thought to himself. There'd be none of that today. Here was an opportunity to share. If he wasn't mistaken, he'd just watched a whole finger of KitKat part company with its owner, and if there is anything that mice love more than anything else, it's a bit of KitKat.

Gatt watched the group intently. They all had their backs to him and seemed to be interested in something on the pitch. The mouse was itching to get his paws on the prize and decided to risk making the short run across the gangway between the seating. He'd be in the open for a matter of seconds. Off he went. In that instant, Titus, who was anything but engrossed in the tour, dropped to his knee to tie his shoelace. Gatt's sudden movement registered in the corner of his eye, and for a moment, man and mini-beast made wide-eyed contact. For a moment, Gatt froze. He watched the boy start to form the word 'MOUSE' and in desperation put a finger to his lips as if to shush him. Titus did a double take. Had a mouse just communicated with him? In a flash, Gatt darted from view. Titus turned back towards the group and lifted an involuntary finger as if to make a point, then checked himself. He decided that perhaps it wasn't a good idea to make a second unwanted interruption to the tour.

'Would you look at that?' Buster Bosch exclaimed. 'I didn't realise the tour included an appearance by the England cricket team captain.'

On the outfield, a tall young man with dark hair was making his way across the outfield. He was smartly dressed in a navy blazer. His slick black hair suggested that he'd just showered.

'Yes, the whole squad is here today for a last net session before their next tour.'

'What are we waiting for? Can we go and have a look?' Buster was getting very excited.

'Oh no, no, no, sir. I'm afraid that is quite out of the question. That sort of thing is carried on behind closed doors. The team's development is strictly confidential.'

Neville was laying it on a bit thick. He enjoyed his little bit of inside knowledge of what happened behind the scenes at Lord's.

'What about if I just hop over the fence here? Any chance I could grab an autograph from the skipper?'

Neville raised an eyebrow that suggested that he might not.

The young man on the outfield, perhaps aware that he was attracting some interest, had made good progress and was just making his way up the steps into the pavilion.

'Eish!' Buster exclaimed. 'Excuse my Afrikaans, but it would have been kinda cool to meet the guys.'

'So near and yet so far,' Neville intoned in a singsong way that was reminiscent of a clergyman recounting a parable. 'Shall we?' he instructed, shooing his flock back down the stairs that took them out of the grandstand.

As they moved away, Gatt blew out his cheeks in relief and retrieved the finger of chocolate. He sniffed down the length of it and let out an approving sigh. He'd followed the tour party farther than he'd usually venture, and he sized up his prize for the return journey. It was easier to eat than transport.

Eventually, he came up with the idea of balancing it on one shoulder. He'd keep it in place with his right forepaw, enabling him to scamper away on three paws. It was a good idea but not being the fittest member of the mouse colony, Gatt soon tired. He sat on his haunches, puffing. It was no good... he'd have to find another way.

He put his precious find down and scurried along the line of seats towards the pavilion. The whole area had been fastidiously swept clean, and there wasn't anything that might be used to transport it. He looked up the stepped seating that rose like an unconquerable mountain above him. He shook his head, definitely too much like hard work. He'd just have to tough it out. He ran back to where he'd left the chocolate, and to his horror, found that a pigeon had spotted it and was making a beeline for it.

'Oh no you don't!' cried Gatt, getting to it and snatching it up in the nick of time. But the pigeon wasn't going to give up without a fight. It landed, or rather crash-landed in a puff of feathers. Picking itself up, the pigeon lurched towards Gatt. The mouse held the finger of KitKat protectively behind him and backed away. The pigeon stepped towards him undaunted and pecked Gatt sharply on the shoulder.

'Oi, OUCH!' Gatt squeaked as the pigeon pecked at him again. 'Will you stop that!' he bellowed as fiercely as he could, but the pigeon was relentless.

To distract it, much as it pained him to do it, Gatt snapped the very end of the chocolate finger and tossed it towards the pigeon. It had the desired effect, and the pigeon flapped over to retrieve it. As it pecked at the morsel, Gatt spotted what had caused the pigeon's quirky landing. A red rubber band had got wrapped around one of its feet and was caught in two of its toes.

Surely here was an opportunity for them both. The band would make a perfect bandolier to wear across his shoulder, and he could thread the KitKat finger into it. But would the pigeon go for it?

He edged towards the bird, which having pecked the chocolate and wafer into fragments was engrossed in hoovering them up. Slowly, Gatt reached out towards the rubber band, and having hooked a paw into it, gave it as hard and sudden a yank as he could muster. This worked until the elasticity of the band took over and returned Gatt to his starting point, and then disconcertingly beyond it. The resulting collision would have been all the better had there been a loud comedy 'BOING' sound, but it had the effect of parting mouse, pigeon and rubber band. The startled bird took flight, and Gatt suddenly found himself alone, the limp rubber band by his side.

'Perfect,' he announced as he slipped it over one shoulder and, having inserted the remainder of the KitKat finger, sped off towards home.

On the other side of the ground, at the door of the pavilion, the president of the MCC, or Marylebone Cricket Club, welcomed the England captain.

'Hello there. Thanks so much for making time for us. Just a word of warning, the old boy is a bit deaf,' the president cupped his hand to his mouth conspiratorially. 'Now, if you'd like to follow me, he's in the Committee Room.'

The president led the way through the Long Room and across the hallway to the Committee Room. In an armchair, swathed in a biscuit-coloured shawl, sat an elderly gentleman. A photographer hovered in the background. He framed a trial photograph through the huge single-pane window overlooking the playing surface. The old man made to get up as the two men entered the room.

'No, no, please don't get up,' the president urged before making the introductions.

'I'd like you to meet Colonel Kulkarni, the Honorary Librarian of the Cricket Club of India.'

The elderly gentleman held out a hand and shook the young captain's hand surprisingly vigorously.

'Colonel Kulkarni has been over from Mumbai taking part in some First World War Centenary Commemorative events.' The MCC president explained. 'He is the son of a soldier who played a part in a remarkable game of cricket that took place behind the battle lines in 1915. A team of soldiers from and Indian Regiment, the 125th Napier Rifles, played a team of English soldiers. I believe a couple on the English side had played county cricket, isn't that right, Colonel.'

The old man nodded confirmation.

'You already know something of the matter, but I should let the colonel tell you more.'

'I'm so pleased to meet you, young man,' Colonel Kulkarni beamed whilst continuing to shake the England captain's hand. 'I'm delighted to have this opportunity to tell you about this unlikely game. A brief respite from horrors that neither you nor I can conceive for those young men on the western front. But on top of that, consider for a moment the plight of the Indian boys. Not only were they far from home, fighting another man's war, but few of them had ever encountered cold weather. Even the summer of 1915 brought little relief, as it was cold and wet. Talk of home and of their love of cricket helped them survive and created a strong bond between them.'

Having managed to wrestle his hand back, the young England captain rubbed his chin thoughtfully. He had one of the toughest, most minutely scrutinized jobs in sport, but it was nothing compared to what these guys had endured.

'I can see you have compassion for these boys,' the old man said as he bobbled his head from side to side. 'So, to the cricket.' He rubbed his hands in anticipation. 'The men would not spend all their time at the front. They would be sent back behind the lines to rest. So it was that two groups of 'brothers' came to play each other in a game of cricket. I say "brothers" because although they came from many miles apart, fate had brought them to that terrible place to fight side by side.'

'During that summer of 1915, while those young men were recuperating, plans were being made for what would be known as the Battle of Loos. It was important to keep morale up, and sport was seen as a good way to try and combat the terrible stress the men endured.' The old man tutted and shook his head, lost in thought for a moment. 'Well, you can imagine that when there was an opportunity for a spot of cricket, the Indian soldiers leapt at the chance.'

'So it was that an England side built around a couple of county players took on an enthusiastic team of Indian jawans, or young soldiers. Of course, they had no square to speak of and a rough and rutted outfield I should imagine, so I cannot attest to the quality of the cricket. Little information has survived about the game to tell the truth, other than that they played for a small trophy. My father told me it was in the form of a little wooden elephant. Presumably one of the men had taken it out to France as a lucky charm.'

The president looked at his watch. Colonel Kulkarni was a lovely old boy, but he wasn't the world's speediest storyteller, and the president was aware that the England captain's time was precious.

'Despite the hardship these men had endured, they had not lost their sense of humour,' Kulkarni continued. 'What do you think they called this trophy?'

'Err... Ellie?' the England captain ventured weakly.

'No, the 'Bombay Duck Trophy!' The old man held his sides and rocked in his chair with mirth. 'It's really very good, don't you think?'

Plainly, the blank face that met this explanation suggested he didn't.

'Wait, now I see the problem. Bombay is the old name for the city of Mumbai and 'duck', well we've all had plenty of those in our time,' he explained, chuckling again. 'But some joker carved it on the trophy with a gap, so it read 'BOMB-ay DUCK' in recognition of their predicament in the trenches.'

Both his listeners 'Aaah-ed' their comprehension.

'So who won in the end?' asked the MCC president.

'Not the Germans!' the old man snorted. He was beginning to enjoy his day out. 'Who won, you ask? I'm afraid, as with the score of the Christmas Day football match of 1914, nobody can remember. It is that the game took place at all that is to be celebrated. My father recounted a sort of bash and dash game among friends. Everyone had a good time and forgot, for an afternoon at least, why they were there.'

'And the trophy?'

'Disappeared into the quagmire of the battlefield I can only imagine. However, it is the sportsmanship and spirit of those boys that we are here to salute.'

'Of course, and we're delighted to be able to help out at with the Centenary Game that you've masterminded in Mumbai,' the

MCC president enthused.

'I cannot thank you enough for your help. It is truly wonderful that you have been able to squeeze an extra game into your busy tour.' The colonel held his hands in a prayer position and bowed.

'It's in aid of a fantastic cause, and it'll be good to play an early game to adjust to local conditions,' the young captain said with a smile. 'There can be a lot of sitting around in hotels on tour, so we'll take any opportunity to get out and about.'

'I wish I could be there with you both,' said the president as he waved the photographer over. With that, the meeting of the three men was recorded for posterity.

'It's been very nice to meet you,' the England captain said earnestly, leaning over to shake the old man's hand again.

'The honour is all mine. What a wonderful place to visit.' He squeezed the young man's hand and held it for what seemed an overly long time nodding, eyes closed and smiling. Suddenly he opened his eyes again so wide that the whites of them showed around the entire perimeter of the irises.

'So one hundred years later, our brothers will go head to head again. I urge you to play in the same spirit that those boys did all those years ago. Good Luck to you all and enjoy the cricket. Play hard, play fair and enjoy your tour of India!'

## Chapter Two

'Fast boxing, 1-2-3-4-5. Change bag! Hard boxing 1-2-3-4-5. Change bag!' Compo called the workout routine and Beaky dutifully responded.

This frenzied activity was taking place a few inches below the sedate meeting. In an area newly developed by the pavilion's mouse colony, two of its inhabitants were furiously working out in what can only be described as a mini boxing gym. Five punch bags hung from the ceiling made out of the fingers of a leather glove and filled with cushion stuffing. A collection of skipping ropes hung from a tack on the wall. Along with soft mats for floor exercises, there were dumbbells made out of nuts and bolts and various rubber bands for resistance training. There was even a sort of exercise bike, a rickety contraption cobbled together from some string, a cotton reel and the inner workings of an old stapler. The fitness regime had come about as a result of their scare earlier in the year, and all of them had been working on beefing themselves up. Happily for the mice, the intrusion of the local rat population had been a one off. Now the events of the night of the great cricket match in the Long Room had been consigned to mouse colony folklore.

The mice had beaten their would-be rivals in the game to decide who should live at the world's most famous cricketing address, and measures had been taken to ensure that security was tightened up. The gym area served a double purpose, as it was also a bolthole should they run into any further unwelcome guests. CMJ, the resident statistician and number cruncher, had pinpointed its location right below the Committee Room. Here all sorts of important meetings took place involving important people, and CMJ had warned of the risk. A new tunnel had been started as an escape route. During its excavation, the mice had stumbled across an up until now undiscovered space that served this dual purpose well. Due to the architecture of the building, the tunnel had taken a twisting route with a number of ups and downs and tight squeezes. As such, it provided an excellent getaway route should the need arise. But in creating it, the mice had lost track of the layout of the building. It was decided therefore that the gym should only be used at times when it was unlikely for there to be humans in the vicinity or as a meeting point in an emergency.

'Jab, jab, jab, uppercut, hook!' Compo called. He was unaware that the meeting was taking place above him and that his squeaked commands might be heard.

The mice were not hibernators; they had no need to be with their ready source of food. They were, however, fond of their beds, and for the most part, the inhabitants of the colony were fast asleep. The mouse residence that afternoon was quiet and secure. Beaky and Compo, who were supposed to be keeping watch for any unwanted intruders, had decided that it was probably safe for them to leave their post for a short while. After all, nobody could tell them off for wanting to keep fit. That is unless it is the individual who'd been most particular in setting up the 'look out' rota who discovers you.

As one of the senior members of the colony, Don had felt the rat's intrusion and threat very deeply. He was determined that as long as he was around, everything possible would be done to keep their home safe.

He'd got up early after a restless sleep brought about by a nightmare. In it the local rats had finally succeeded in evicting them from their home. Having wandered down to the pantry for a snack, he'd expected to bump into one of the stationed lookouts. He was horrified to find that not only one, but both had deserted their posts!

From the dining area he scampered down past the cricket practice net hoping to find the two scallywags. There was no sign of them. He carried on to the entrance to the residence. Here an intersection led up to the Long Room and left to the 'thunderbox' entrance that led to the outside world. Following their recent activity, there was now a third option, and Don squeezed himself though the opening. It was tight even for a mouse. He then zigzagged through a series of sharp edges. These had been left by the mice that had undertaken the work of gnawing through the various materials that made up the skeleton of the old building. A long straight section followed which angled deep down under the floorboards, a sharp jag right, then left. It was a twisting route, but that was good, Don thought to himself.

Now he started to climb again. Back at the level of the residence he had to wiggle through another series of layers of wall, skirting and plaster before finally squeezing through the entrance to the safe room. In real terms, he'd passed from beneath the Long Room, through a wall, across a corridor and through the next wall to the Committee Room, but in mouse terms, it was much more of an adventure.

Inside the safe room, the disobedient pair were still in the swing of things. Beaky had moved on to the dumbbells, while Compo was going through his full repertoire at one of the punch bags.

'Look, watch my 'Ali Shuffle',' he called over to Beaky.

Beaky watched opened-mouthed as Compo executed a foot manoeuvre, shuffling his feet backwards and forwards in a dazzling blur. However, before he could comment, he spotted Don standing beside him, arms folded, foot tapping.

'Yeah,' cried Compo. 'I float like a butterfly, sting like a b...' The mouse had performed a neat pirouette that had brought him round to face Don.

'Oh!' he said.

'Oh indeed,' Don replied, clearly irritated.

Beaky, meanwhile, attempted to edge out of Don's view.

'And where do you think you're going?' Don snapped.

Beaky, taken by surprise, dropped his dumbbell. It fell with a metallic clunk before rolling along the floor, knocking over a strip of stainless steel. The makeshift mirror fell with a sickening clang.

The meeting in the Committee Room above had broken up. Having said his goodbyes, the president was just giving the room a last look before leaving for the day.

From beneath the floor, the clang of falling metal could be clearly heard. Its sound registered on his face, elevating one eyebrow several centimetres higher than the other. He pinpointed the spot where the sound had come from and walked a very precise circle over the area, listening intently.

Below the floor, the mice held their breath as they watched small sprinkles of dust fall from between the floorboards above them. The president crouched on all fours and put an ear to the floor. There wasn't a sound from below. Satisfied that there was to be no more of whatever it had been, the president retrieved his mobile phone from his jacket and dialled a number.

Beneath the floorboards, Don motioned the other two mice back towards the main residence, and the three scuttled off.

'What on earth were you thinking?' scolded Don when they were back under the Long Room.

Compo and Beaky looked downcast and fidgeted nervously.

'Think about it, guys. Just a few weeks ago, we nearly lost everything. And why was that? Because of uninvited visitors, that's why. Who's to say that it won't happen again? We have to be vigilant at all times however safe things seem. I don't know about you, but I certainly don't want to find myself scraping by goodness knows where.'

'Sorry, Don,' said Compo sheepishly.

'We won't let it happen again,' Beaky chipped in.

'You're too right it won't!' Don wasn't ready to soften his stance yet, and he stomped off, leaving the atmosphere charged.

Beaky's face was a picture of concern as he watched his friend walk away.

'He'll calm down in a bit, you wait and see,' Compo reasoned, clapping a paw round his friend's shoulder.

'I do hope so; I hate it when there's a falling out,' said Beaky glumly.

Meanwhile, the president's call rang in Mr Hobbs', the Clerk of Works at the ground, office. James McCrackers, ex-professional cricketer, Marylebone Cricket Club eccentric and general 'moocher around' was with him. He was sitting at the desk opposite Mr Hobbs, his feet propped on its top and a bag of jelly babies balanced on his tummy.

'Who is it?' he mouthed to Mr Hobbs.

Mr Hobbs shushed him with a shake of his head.

'Yes, sir, I quite understand. If you're worried there has been another infestation, we'd better bring forward our fortnightly visit and get the people in.'

Other sporting arenas in and around London had other problems to contend with. At Twickenham, for example, a falcon is flown around the space once a week. The idea being that the local pigeon fraternity get used to the fact that there is a bird of prey in the area and it acts as a natural deterrent. Victorian buildings in central London like the Lord's Pavilion, however, attract a different sort of uninvited guest. From time to time, the mice would give themselves away. Then they'd be subjected to a tiresome round of traps, poisons and general interference to their way of life.

'Don't tell me those little cheeky little critters have put in another appearance!' McCrackers boomed as Mr Hobbs put the telephone down.

'I don't know,' Mr Hobbs said wearily. 'Maybe they have, maybe they haven't. All I know is that the chief chap thinks he heard something, so better get the Pest Arrest boys in to have a shufti.'

McCrackers had mixed feelings about the mice. It had been him who'd ensured that they keep their home, having intervened to save them from rats. He had frightened them off when they'd refused to accept the result of the cricket match played to decide who should have the right to live beneath the pavilion. As a result, he felt a certain fondness towards them.

'Are you sure that's entirely necessary?'

'You know what a fusspot El Presidente can be.'

Their discussion was interrupted by a tremendous rumbling sound outside the office, and both men moved over to the window to investigate. Outside, an elderly dark green tractor, known affectionately as 'Ivor the engine', was trundling round the circumference of the stadium. It was pulling behind it a clanking trailer piled high with blue kit bags.

'Oh heavens, I'd forgotten all about that,' burst out Mr Hobbs.

'What, that the England cricket team is going on tour?' McCrackers stuttered in disbelief.

'Given the fact that they've been around the place for days practicing, I think not,' Mr Hobbs said wearily. 'No, I said I'd make sure that the pavilion doors are open so that Terry Packer, the 'kit man', can stow it all in the Long Room. There's so much of it, and it makes it easy for him to double check that it's all there before the off tomorrow.'

'Fascinating,' murmured McCrackers, clearly not fascinated.

'Shouldn't you be somewhere else?' I've got things to do you know, and I'd like to lock my office up if I'm heading out,' said Mr Hobbs, shooing McCrackers out.

At the pavilion doors, Terry was clearly twitchy when Mr Hobbs jogged up. He tapped an imaginary watch on his wrist.

'I'm so sorry, Terry. I was waylaid by Mr McCrackers. What can I say?' it was a slightly unkind half-truth, but it was an excuse that had such wide-ranging connotations that it needed no further explanation.

'No worries, I know what the old fella can be like.'

Terry was an unflappable Australian. It was slightly ironic that he should be in charge of kitting out the England cricket team given the two nations sporting rivalry. However, when it came to the ordering, branding and the distribution of 500 or so separate pieces of cricket clothing, he was the man. Not only that, but also then rounding up the bags of the players once they added their own bits and bobs. Add to these the players' 'coffins', the gruesomely named huge bags packed with their particular brands of bats, pads, gloves, shoes and helmets. The number of bags was truly astounding, and organising the movement of all this stuff from one country to another was a task of military proportions.

Terry and Mr Hobbs were soon joined by a party of players from the club's Young Cricketers' programme. The youngsters made light work of transporting the bags into the Long Room and arranging them like lines of big blue sausages down the length of the room.

Terry worked his way among them, clipboard in hand, checking what was there and to whom it belonged. Eventually, he was satisfied that everything was in place.

'Righto, Mr Hobbs, that seems to be just about it. We'll all be back again tomorrow morning to put in on the transport to the airport.'

'No problem at all. I'll be here bright and early.'

With that, the doors to the pavilion were fastened. There were no functions that evening, and all around the ground computers were being turned off and offices closed. Lights started to glow around the ground as the sun went down.

Gatt was relieved to make it back before it got too dark. He'd travelled much farther than he'd have liked, and he was feeling the effects of his exertions. In fact, he felt so tired that he'd had to have to a small snack and a short snooze part way home. As he neared home, he found that a carpenter had removed a post from a wooden staircase to repair at one end of the pavilion. It had left a hole, which he'd made his way through. To his delight, it brought him straight into the main part of the building but at floor level rather than just below it. Having squeezed under the doors at the end of the Long Room, he'd been about to slip beneath the floorboards when he'd noticed the lines of shadowy bags. They looked like a range of mountains stretching away from him. The mice had seen them before, and it was a source of excitement—the idea that *the* equipment of *the* England cricket team was just sitting there inches above their home.

A little while later, back in the colony, he was excitedly explaining to anyone who'd listen how he'd retrieved the piece of KitKat as a treat for everyone. Also that he'd discovered that the England players' belongings were in the Long Room above them.

'There'll be no chocolate for breakfast,' Mrs Heyhoe cautioned. 'Anyway, it looks like you've eaten most of it.'

'What do you mean?' Gatt whined plaintively.

'I can see it stuck to your whiskers.'

Not much escaped Mrs Heyhoe's notice. She had a knack of knowing just about everything that was going on, when and where, within the colony.

'I had to give some of it to a pigeon,' Gatt explained.

'Maybe he got it *cheep*!' Bumble, who'd been eavesdropping on their conversation, chipped in.

'Very funny,' Gatt groaned. 'I wish I hadn't bothered now. Risking life and limb. Walking all that way... I only wanted to give the little ones a treat.'

'Well, I'll see that it gets divided up and shared amongst them,' said Mrs Heyhoe, whisking away what was left of the chocolate finger.

Other members of the colony had started to join them. With less to scavenge in the winter months, there was a fairer split in looking after the children. A number of the ladies were sitting at a long table in the dining area while their husbands were tending to the children. As night fell, some of the children had started to wake.

The events of the past summer had brought what was already a tight community even closer together. Before there had been the odd little group that kept itself to itself, but now there was a wholehearted communal feel, and the dining area was its heart.

'It is such a relief to have a break from the cricket,' Mrs WG observed casually.

A small, unseen shockwave ran the length of the table.

'There are worse hobbies,' Mrs Beaky, who was quite fond of cricket, replied.

'Given where we live, I don't think we're ever going to get away from it completely,' Mrs Beefy pointed out wisely.

'Don't get me wrong. There are all sorts of good things about the game. It's just that I quite like it when the season has ended. Life is a little more relaxed for everyone.'

'It would be nice to go on a holiday somewhere exotic,' Mrs Ranji said dreamily.

'Well, I for one am keen to stay put. There was quite enough trouble about going elsewhere with those horrid rats.' Mrs Beaky shivered at the memory.

A gaggle of children arrived followed by their fathers.

'Dad says that the England team's bags are upstairs. Can we go and have a look at them? Can we please?'

'Just you sit down and have your breakfast, you little monkeys.' Mrs Heyhoe had arrived and tried to settle everyone down.

However, the children were excited, and several of them chipped in with requests of their own.

'Hey, hey now, what's all this?' Don enquired as he joined the group.

The clamour of requests started again.

'All right everyone. Let's quieten down,' Don asked, holding his paws up to calm them down. 'After breakfast, I'll make a plan with some of the dads to take you up in small groups to have a look. How does that sound?'

There was a shrill cheer of 'HOORAY' followed by vigorous shushing of everyone by the adults.

'Well, I'm sure not all the girls will want to go,' said Mrs WG. 'I'll take those that don't want to go for a play in the nursery, which will make it easier for everyone.' After her earlier comment, she didn't want to be seen as a party-pooper, and this way she could help everyone out.

It was decided that the children should be taken up in small groups each led by two adults. They'd be able to have a run around and a peep inside the bags before returning to the residence. The adult males were paired up, and Mikey and Knotty set off with the first group of excited little ones.

Don was twitchy all the time they were gone. He didn't like it when groups of the children headed to the surface. They were easily excited and their behaviour could be unpredictable, particularly if faced with a sudden threat.

'Cheer up, mate, it might never happen.' Beefy had wandered up and ruffled the fur on the top of Don's head in an effort to cheer him up.

'Do you mind?' Don snapped at him before catching himself.

'Sorry, old chum, but you know I'm always nervous about the youngsters going out.'

'They'll be fine. The place is empty and all the humans will be tucked up nice and cosy in their homes. They're not as daft as we like to think they are, you know.'

As the two mice chuckled, the first party made its way back into the residence. The children were bubbling with enthusiasm.

'How was it?' Beefy asked them as the bounded in.

'There were so many bags, and they were enormous! The dads helped us up and we had a look in one,' stammered one.

'Yeah, and Dad showed us the wicketkeeper's gloves!' cried Little Knotty.

'Poo, they were so smelly,' his little sister added.

'But so cool to think that they were the actual England wicketkeeper's gloves,' he said dreamily.

'Who's going up next?' Compo asked.

'Certainly not you, or you,' Don broke in, addressing Compo and Beaky. 'In fact, you two should be getting some shut-eye, as you're going to be doubling up on your watch duty.'

'But we'll be able to go up and have a look later, won't we?'

'No, you will not!' Don said sharply. He was still smarting from their perceived disloyalty to the colony in leaving their posts.

'Surely we could go up later,' Compo pleaded.

But Don would hear nothing of it. 'You can do the last two hours up until sunrise.'

'He's kidding, right?' Compo pleaded to those around him.

Don certainly wasn't listening and had padded away to help sort out the next group to go up to the Long Room.

'He sounded pretty serious to me.' Beaky stepped up, looking downcast.

'You're not the boss. You can't tell me what to do!' Compo called after Don.

'Steady on now, lad. I think everyone knows the pecking order down here,' Fred warned.

But Compo wasn't listening. Instead he stomped off towards the sleeping quarters. Willow was coming out of her bat-making workshop as he passed and was surprised when he ignored her hello. Beaky had chased after him.

'Don't mind him, Willow, he's just a bit upset,' he said apologising for his friend before going after him again.

When Beaky caught up with him, he found that Compo had flopped on his bed moodily.

'Let's get some kip,' Beaky suggested. 'Things will look more sunny after a sleep.'

But Compo remained tight-lipped.

'Have it your own way,' Beaky sighed. 'I'm off to my own bed. I'll come and get you up later.'

In truth, the mice were tired, and as the rest of the colony went about their nocturnal activities, they slept.

He'd slept so soundly, Beaky could hardly believe it when Knotty woke him. He did so with a gentle shake and a soft 'Wakey, wakey'. He collected Compo, who seemed in better spirits, and the two scuttled off and settled at their posts. Beaky had brought them each a pine nut as a snack and a distraction. Compo was a fidget by nature, and he found that the time passed slowly.

'Oi, Beaky,' he called to his friend, who was a little way down the passage from the entrance to the residence. 'Why is it that when you're having fun, time zips by? Then when you're doing something a little more mind numbing, it grinds to a halt.'

'I wouldn't let Don hear you talk like that...' The sound of someone approaching stopped him short.

'H-h-halt! Who goes there?' Beaky asked, suddenly spooked.

'Don't mind me,' said a voice.

'Bumble!' Beaky exclaimed. 'You nearly gave me heart failure.'

'That's a nice welcome, I must say, for your dear old Bumble.

Who, out of the kindness of his heart, has popped down to take you guys up to have a look around upstairs.'

'Really? Are you serious?' Beaky said in disbelief.

'Yes. As Gatt's on duty next, he's going to stand in for you. But mum's the word, eh? It can be our little secret.'

Compo didn't need telling twice. Having thanked Gatt for his part in their mischief, the three mice made their way up above the floorboards to the Long Room. The sun was just starting to come up, and the first hint of daylight peaked through the windows of the Long Room.

'Oh my goodness, how cool is this?' Compo cried as he romped up to the first of the bags lined up along the floor. 'Give me a leg up one of you.'

Bumble and Beaky did as requested.

'Don't you want to look in a particular player's bag?' Bumble asked, his voice muffled by the fact that Compo was using his snout as a foothold.

'Nah,' Compo called down, stretching his paws out to help pull up his mates. 'They all have the same stuff, I think you'll find.'

The mice skipped along the length of the blue England team bag hauling the tab of the zip. As it opened, a waft of newness seeped out of it.

'Ooh I love all that new kit,' Compo rubbed his paws together and dived into the bag.

'Well, if you can't beat 'em, join 'em,' declared Bumble as he leapt into the void.

'Hey, fellas, hold up!' Beaky looked into depths of the bag from the edge. 'Oh crumbs,' he said as he looked nervously over his shoulder before following them in.

Compo

Beaky

## Chapter Three

The day had not started well for Spike Smith. He'd had to get up horribly early and the hot water in his home had yet to come on. The brief lukewarm shower had, however, given him the jolt required to get him up, out and on the road. As a professional driver, the quiet time before the London rush hour started was a joy. He'd picked his coach up in South London and driven into the centre of town, taking in some of his favourite landmarks. Over Lambeth Bridge, round Parliament Square and down Whitehall. He saluted as he drove past the cenotaph—his dad had told him this was the done thing as a boy, and he'd done it ever since. Past Nelson in Trafalgar Square, Hyde Park Corner and the Duke of Wellington's No.1 London address. Along Park Lane and a glimpse of the 'super car' showrooms he'd visit if he won the lottery. By the time he reached the Grace Gates at Lord's Cricket Ground, he'd had a sightseeing tour that would have delighted any visitor.

Sid Pickett, the gate attendant, had also had an early start and greeted Spike with a wave. As the regular driver for the team bus, Spike knew the ropes. He'd load up the bags before heading off to collect the team from their hotel. Once he'd rounded up the team and its entourage, he'd whisk them out to the west of London and Heathrow Airport.

'Very prompt, Spike,' Sid complimented him. 'I'll get the gates open but just you mind my gate posts, you know what a tight squeeze it is.'

'I'll breathe in, don't you worry,' Spike joked, sucking in his cheeks to make himself look as thin as possible.

In truth, Spike was skilled at his job. He spun the coach round as if it were a small family car and backed it in through the narrow gates, then all the way up to the rear doors of the pavilion. Here they met Mr Hobbs, whose day hadn't gone entirely to plan. He'd overslept, but as he'd only had to nip round the corner from his house on the grounds, he was still wearing his pyjamas. They were red and yellow striped, the colours of the Marylebone Cricket Club. He'd pulled on a purple sweater with a green diamond pattern on the front and stuffed his feet into his laced work shoes before sprinting round the ground.

'That's quite a look!' Spike observed, rubbing his chin thoughtfully.

'Wish I'd worn my sunglasses,' Sid added.

'Ahem, yes, sorry. Bit of a mess up on the alarm clock front,' Mr Hobbs coughed.

'We're glad you made it, just hope the CCTV cameras don't turn you into a YouTube sensation.'

Mr Hobbs looked at his reflection in the glass of the door nervously.

'Shall we...?' Spike gestured towards the pavilion.

Inside their chosen bag, the mice were very excited. They'd found a coveted real England test cap. Normally, the players were very cautious about where they kept these and liked to keep them in their possession. Number 647, however, had obviously decided that it was safe enough amongst all the other gear. The mice were just trying to make the number out and whom it might belong to when the light from the open zip suddenly disappeared. Mr Hobbs had walked the length of the kit bags, and seeing one unzipped, he'd simply closed it, unwittingly sealing the mice inside.

'Ooer,' Beaky whispered.

'Hmm, ooer indeed,' replied Bumble.

'What now?' Compo added, which was more to the point.

As the three mice contemplated their predicament, they felt the bag jolt upwards. For an instant, they felt the sensation of flying and then a thump. Mr Hobbs had picked the bag up by its handles and swung it over his shoulder.

Out of the Long Room they flew, descending a short flight of stairs before landing with a bump as the bag was deposited on the ground. Within seconds, they were up in the air again, another bump and more movement as the bag was slid into one of the side lockers of the coach.

Inside the bag, the mice had braced themselves in little star shapes hoping that they'd be able to ride out their turbulent journey. It was fortunate for them that most of the contents of the cricket bags had been designed to provide protection, and so they remained unscathed.

'I think we've left the building,' Bumble announced.

'Thank you, Elvis,' Compo remarked, managing to find some humour in what was a pretty dire situation.

'We will be all right, won't we?' Beaky said nervously, seeking some sort of reassurance from his friends.

But before anyone could answer, the sides of the bag started to move inwards. As Spike loaded more bags onto the coach he squashed them up against each other. As he did so, it seemed that with every additional bag, the odds of the mice getting crushed were getting worse.

'Quick!' cried Compo. 'Find the batting helmet, it will be at one end.'

The three mice snaked their way through the layers of clothing to one end of the bag.

'It's not at this end. Back up, boys,' Bumble urged.

Beaky was thoroughly freaked out by now and shot to the other end of bag. The other two followed him and both heard a hollow 'doink' as Beaky struck the hard hat with his noggin.

'Sounds like 'e's found it,' Bumble smirked.

Beaky had stunned himself and had slumped by the helmet.

'Quick, take his arm and help me get him inside,' Compo ordered. The two mice bundled their friend through the metal grill at the front of the helmet to safety.

'Crikey that was close,' Compo gasped as the arrival of another bag caused them to be buffeted about beneath the helmet.

Eventually there was a loud metallic clunk, some human voices and then the sound of the engine starting up. By now Beaky had come round.

'Were leaving our home, aren't we?' he said sadly.

'We are, old son,' Bumble's tone was unusually serious.

'Where are we going?'

'Well, you can look at this as either a good or a bad thing, but it appears that we're going on tour with the England cricket team,' Compo stated what to him seemed fairly obvious.

Back at their home, it was too early for the stowaways to be missed. The other mice beneath the Long Room remained blissfully unaware that three of their friends were being driven away through the Grace Gates.

Things were less calm for the three extra passengers hidden amongst the luggage. It seemed as though the coach driver was deliberately making the ride as lumpy as possible as they lurched from one side to another. They clung to the grill of the helmet, being swung to and fro as if they were on a fairground ride. However, no sooner had they got used to the movement of the vehicle than it came to a halt. Spike had driven them only as far as a nearby hotel where the team members were awaiting his arrival.

The players drifted out of the building's entrance. Some zoned out wearing headphones, others engrossed in their phones and a couple of the more boyish members of the party horsing around. They had the appearance of a party on a school trip all kitted out in identical regulation team suits. Behind them came a small army of support staff, coaches of this and that, medical staff and the team management. More luggage arrived with them, and once again the side lockers of the coach were opened.

'Can you hear that?' Beaky said from the depths of the bag. 'It sounds like they're getting us out.'

Further buffeting of their bag suggested otherwise, and the slamming shut of the doors sometime later confirmed it. Soon they were back on the road, and having negotiated the residential streets of St John's Wood, their driver headed west.

Now on a straight road, the mice were able to relax, and they huddled together beneath the helmet. Sleep enveloped them and thoughts of their predicament drifted away with it.

In the morning, the bulk of the London rush hour traffic comes in from the west. Travelling in the opposite direction, the coach made good time. The mice had been lulled by its smooth passage, but their reprieve didn't last long. Soon they were very much awake again, woken by the groan of the luggage locker doors opening again.

They could hear voices, instructions given and then a shushing, sliding sound and movement. Yes, a definite sensation of movement. Uh-oh, flying again. Was that a good thing? *Thump!* The heavy landing suggested not as the mice were tossed about beneath the helmet.

As the first bag on, they were the last off. They were placed on the top of a large baggage trolley that had been piled with the other bags. Fortunately, the mice were unaware that now they were precariously balanced on a bag mountain, a fall from which would be damaging to say the least. A porter laid a restraining hand on their bag to secure it as if he knew its cargo was particularly vulnerable. A colleague joined him, and together they manhandled the trolley into the airport terminal.

The mice now had to endure a seemingly endless wait while each of the tour party had their personal bags weighed and tagged. After this, they were fed onto a conveyer belt on which they disappeared into the inner workings of the airport.

Still waiting to be processed, the mice sat tense in their bag, awaiting their next ordeal. None of them spoke. Any optimism they'd had about their situation at the beginning of the journey had been literally been knocked out of them.

'Okay, if you'd like to bring the big trolley over,' an airline 'check-in' girl at the bag drop counter instructed.

Terry Packer the team 'kit man' pushed the trolley over. It was one of those instances when a person's name fits their job although not quite in the same league as Mark De Man, the Belgian footballer.

'Can you tell me what's in each bag?'

'Every bag is packed with the same amount of clothing. There should be four pairs of cricket trousers, two floppy hats, a jacket, six different shirts, some shorts, tracksuits and a couple of sweaters. Then there are the players' cricket bags. All those will be slightly different,' Terry explained.

'Could we have a look in one so that I can have an idea?' the girl asked.

Terry grabbed the top bag and set it down on the weigh scale by the girl's feet. As he unzipped it, light flooded into the space the mice occupied. The three of them blinked in surprise, trying to adjust to the sudden change in their surroundings.

'So everyone has a slightly different way of packing them, pads on top or bats on top for example, but essentially it's all the same sort of stuff.' Terry held up a bat that he'd pulled out for the girl to examine.

'Okay, if you could just remove some of the other items so I can see what's right at the bottom.'

Terry did as she asked and grabbed the helmet by the peak. As it started to move, Compo and Bumble sensed the danger. They scuttled out from under it, scrabbling under whatever they could to avoid detection. Beaky, however, had clung to the helmet's lining and was now on an upward trajectory. Terry held the helmet up, and for an instant Beaky had a panoramic view of Heathrow Terminal 5's departure area. The girl looked into the bag and seemed satisfied that everything was as Terry had described.

'Okay, if you'd like to put everything back, then you can start putting them on the conveyor.'

Beaky hung on grimly and returned to the bag. As Terry stuffed the helmet into the end of the bag, the three mice reconvened beneath it. Once it was zipped up, Terry plonked it on the conveyor. The girl fastened a label to it marked with the letters 'BOM' and with a push of a button despatched it to a part of the airport usually unseen by the general public.

That unseen path would take three minutes from check-in to loading bay. It was a long winding journey along a conveyor belt system, a motorway for suitcases, fed by ramps from other check-in desks. A series of ups and downs, twists, turns and bumps, a mazy super highway of intertwined chutes and carousels. Through a security screening system that revealed three small glowing skeletons in one end of one bag. Then a criss-cross net of laser beams that read the barcode on the tag marked 'BOM' and sent the bag to the appropriate area. A special barcode on the team's bags, however, ensured that they received VIP treatment, overriding the automated system. This sent them to an area where a piece of equipment known as a 'human being' actually manhandled the bags off the conveyor, setting them aside to be stowed in a separate part of the aircraft. The bags were to be placed in one of the temperature controlled cargo bins.

Amongst the bags also destined for this area was a large cream plastic crate with a wire mesh door. Inside it lay the slumbering mass of Bonzo, a large sedated dog of indeterminate breed. His owner had first found him as a puppy when he worked with an aid agency in Cambodia. Then he was a brown sinewy pup. Now he was an enormous muscular hound who was not fond of his plastic crate. Sedation had been the only way to get him in it, and the vet's parting words had been... *'I've given him enough medication to stop a charging elephant.'*

Certainly it had had desired effect, and Bonzo was happily reposing in the land of nod. He was certainly oblivious the 'oohs' and 'ahhs' of the baggage handler as he moved the last of the team's luggage. He checked the number of bags against a sheet on a clipboard and signed the note with a flourish. His job done for the moment, he nipped off for a well-deserved break.

A calm descended on the baggage area. The various sounds of the airport echoed in the distance, but for now, the only immediate sound was that of Bonzo's snoring. Inside their bag, the mice sat tight and waited. It was some time before one of them spoke.

'Sounds like we're there,' Beaky whispered hopefully.

'Don't be daft. They're hardly going to go to all this trouble for a drive across town,' Compo reprimanded him slightly unkindly.

'Let's not be horrible to one another,' Bumble said, taking on the role of parent. 'Right now, it sounds pretty quiet outside, so I reckon we should have a look to see just where we are.'

The three made their way up through the contents of the bag. A bat handle had got jammed in the zip, stopping it from being closed completely. Compo popped his head out through the gap first and had a look around.

'Looks like the coast is clear,' he called down to his chums.

Soon all three of them were sitting in a line on top of the bag. At one end of the line, Beaky's tummy rumbled noisily.

He pressed his paws against his tummy to silence it. 'Sorry about that, guys, but, I'm *so* hungry.'

'I'm sure we'll find something before too long,' Bumble said reassuringly.

'Look over there, that looks hopeful,' an eagle eyed Compo observed.

On the floor by Bonzo's crate was a paper sack labelled 'Doggy Dinner' with a picture of a dog eating from a bowl on it.

'That should do the trick. Bumble, you keep a look out, and Beaky and I will go and stock up,' Compo took control.

Together Compo and Beaky skipped down from the bag and scuttled across the floor to the sack of dried dog food. Meanwhile, Bumble sat back on his haunches and scanned the horizon for any potential threat.

At its base, Compo and Beaky sniffed around the bag. A promising smell seeped through its thick paper. Immediately the pair got to work chewing. Beaky was warming to his task, tearing at the paper and spitting small fragments to the floor when Compo put a restraining paw on his shoulder.

'Dog,' he said simply.

'I know, but don't worry about it, it's just a picture.'

'No, a *real* dog,' he motioned sideways with a nod of his head.

Beaky peered round the edge of the bag and visibly jumped as he came face to face with Bonzo.

'My goodness yes, he is a big fellow, isn't he?' Compo voiced Beaky's unuttered thoughts.'

Carefully the two mice approached the grill of Bonzo's crate.

'He's sleeping like a baby,' Beaky observed in a whisper.

"Puppy' don't you mean,' Compo corrected with a smirk.

Bonzo's great leathery nose was pushed up against the grill. Beaky couldn't resist and tentatively reached up to touch it. It was dry and rough.

'I thought dogs were supposed to have wet noses.'

Compo edged closer and gently touched the dog's nose.

'Ooh yes, that *is* dry. Poor thing must need a drink. Tell you what, you keep going on the sack, and I'll get Bumble to help me find some water.'

Beaky got back to work and Compo scampered back to Bumble.

'Psst! Bumble.'

'What can I do you for, young sir?' Bumble called down to his companion, deliberately scrambling the words to make a joke.

'We need a drink for a dog in the crate over here. We think he's dehydrated.'

'What's that you say? A dog? Oh heck, I don't like the sound of that.'

'He's fast asleep. Don't panic.'

'What's 'e want water fer then?' Bumble's Lancashire accent became more pronounced.

'Look, will you help us or not?' Compo asked impatiently.

'There's a bottle on the desk over there.' He pointed towards a half-empty plastic bottle sitting on the baggage handle's desk. 'I did have my eye on it for us.'

'We'll worry about us later,' Compo said decisively.

Once he'd been told, Bumble didn't hesitate in performing a mission impossible style journey to get to the desktop. This involved several death-defying leaps to and from precarious perches and a spiralling climb up a telephone handset cord. Once he'd reached the bottle, he gently pushed it off the desk in the direction of Compo.

The bottle hit the floor, bounced, cracking the screw top and rolled across the floor. Compo retrieved it, rolling it in front of him as if performing a circus trick.

'Watch out, you're spilling it!' Beaky cried.

'Spilling it! I'll spill you,' Compo puffed as he reached the front of Bonzo's crate. 'Now give me a hand to tip it.'

Bonzo's tongue was lolling out of the side of his mouth. Using Beaky as a pivot Compo tipped the bottle up. The water glugged to one end of the bottle and started to trickle out through the cracked top. Bonzo's tongue remained motionless as the water splashed off it. The mice continued to administer their first aid, and suddenly, Bonzo raised himself up from his prone position with a loud slobbering sound, a stretch and a toothy yawn. No sooner was he up than he was down again. The dog crashed back down in his crate and resumed snoring.

'I think he's okay,' Beaky observed.

'I guess so,' Compo replied. 'Now let's get some of that grub and get back to Bumble before the man gets back.'

On the floor was one of the baggage handler's discarded blue latex gloves. Compo scooped it up.

'Here, we can use a couple of the fingers as sacks.'

Each of the mice tore off a finger and stuffed it with as much dried dog food pellets as they could before scrambling back to join Bumble.

As the last mouse-tail disappeared back inside the kit bag a door opened and the baggage handler returned to his post. He bent down in front of Bonzo's crate.

'There's a good boy,' he said in a funny *'the way people talk to dogs'* voice. 'Look at you, you're all wet.' The bottle had rolled away to one side. The man picked it up and looked at it. 'Silly me, must have knocked the bottle off the table.'

But Bonzo was oblivious to his fussing. He was chasing cats or burying bones in a faraway dreamland.

Elsewhere in the airport, the people were working their way through the system. The players had various media commitments. Those complete, they'd been whisked past queues, had their own security check and enjoyed the hospitality of the airline lounge. Now they were passing through the last gate before boarding the aircraft. Prior to this, they'd managed to stay well clear of Morgan Smirk, columnist for *Big Cricket Monthly*.

'Here come the pampered players,' he scoffed with his nose in the air. 'I'm afraid you'll have to wait your turn. I'm ahead of you in the queue.'

But actually he wasn't. An Indian man who appeared to be wearing solid gold sunglasses and sporting an elaborately coiffured hairstyle had taken Morgan Smirk's momentary distraction as an opportunity to squeeze ahead of him.

'Err... excu...u...use me, there is a queue you know.'

Almost instantaneously a monster posing as a personal assistant stepped in and laid a spade-sized hand on Smirk's shoulder.

'Don't mind, don't mind,' the brilliantly bouffant man said quickly. 'I can wait.'

So wait he did while Morgan Smirk self-importantly

negotiated the final embarkation check before being consigned to the last seat at the back of the plane.

The mice were heading for a far more salubrious portion of the plane. Bonzo, who was being shipped as cargo, would be travelling in the climate-controlled section. The team's VIP baggage was consigned to the same area for ease of access at their destination. The mice were now getting used to the process of a sudden relocation. They'd left the building having been loaded onto another baggage trailer. A whole host of sounds assaulted their senses accompanied by the strong smell of aviation fuel. Their little train of trailers snaked its way across the Heathrow tarmac to a waiting aircraft. As the pre-flight jet engine wheeze filled the air, the bags were loaded onto a conveyor and the intrepid trio disappeared into the cargo hold.

There they sat in the darkness of the kit bag as the hulk that housed them clunked and clanked its way through the minutes before departure. Then, without warning, they were on the move.

'At last,' sighed Compo, breaking the silence.

'I wanna stay at home,' Beaky wailed.

'Too late for that I fear, old chum,' Bumble chipped in.

The plane moved slowly at first before building to a more fluent roll. But no sooner had they started than they came to a full stop. A moment's wait, then a lurch forward and a sharp turn.

'I'd wish they'd make up their mind which way they're going,' Bumble said in the darkness.

But the captain and his crew had done just that. As they were cleared for take-off over their headsets, the pilot applied full power and released the brakes. The aircraft's acceleration was rapid and the engine noise became disconcertingly loud. Down the runway they bowled, their speed building and building.

In their hiding place, the three friends edged closer together into a tight huddle. Just when the tension became unbearable, the pilot raised the nose and the plane left the runway en route to Mumbai.

Bumble

## Chapter Four

If you are in the most populated city, in the second-most populated country in the world, finding some personal space is going to be tricky. If you are in the most crowded place, within that most crowded place, then you might as well throw in the towel.

The Dharavi slum is a city within a mega city, a thriving square mile of industry and home to over a million self-sufficient people. Despite these odds, among the narrow lanes of the vibrant community, the mice of the Dharavi mouse cricket team had managed to find a discrete corner to play. It was match day at the Wankhede Cricket Stadium some seven miles south of them. The cricket-loving community of Dharavi had downed tools and were glued to any television they could find. It was due to this fact that the mice had arranged a friendly match against the mice from Mahim Junction. A game to showcase the talent of their home-grown superstar.

Mr Ajit Googly had braved the considerable journey from his home. Travelling in the tiffin box of the conductor of the Bombay Electric Supply Bus had taken some planning, and its execution some derring-do. But he'd made it, much to the surprise and delight of the Dharavi team. The reason for this was that Mr Googly was the chairman of selectors for the celebrated Bombay Yacht Club (Mouse XI.) He had it in his power to make a cricketer's dreams come true, and when it came to cricket dreams, there were none bigger than those of the Dharavi boys.

On his arrival, they'd made a great fuss of Mr Googly.

'Take some tea please,' suggested one.

'Perhaps a small piece of jalebi?' asked another.

'Thank you, no, I've already eaten.' Mr Googly thought back to the delicious dhosa he'd helped himself to in the conductor's tiffin box. 'May we get on with the matter in hand? I have a long way to go, and I'm not sure how I'm going to get home yet,' he said bleakly.

The mice had set up a rough pitch under a giant water pipe. It was a little shady, but this also provided them with some extra security. The mice from Mahim Junction had agreed to take the field for the purposes of Mr Googly's analysis. They were busy going through some fielding practice, throwing the ball into their wicketkeeper at one end of the pitch. The Dharavi team were scattered about the boundary chatting in little groups.

'Shall we begin?' Mr Googly clapped his paws and brought everyone to order. The Mahim players took their fielding positions and the opening bowler paced out his run up. One of the Dharavi openers prised himself from his group of friends and walked part of the way out to the simple wicket. He stopped and looked back towards a little group of mice beyond the boundary. Like a trainer and 'corner men' at a boxing match, they huddled round, flapping, gesticulating and offering advice. At last they parted, revealing a tiny, startled-looking brown mouse in kit several sizes too big for him.

'I can't, Uncle,' he pleaded, seemingly glued to the spot.

'Sure you can, think of it as a knockabout. Anyway, what about all the practice you've put in?' A kindly looking older mouse cooed over him and patted his shoulder.

'You can practice and practice, but the real thing will always be different.'

'Nonsense, now go,' Uncle urged. 'You've got your bat.'

'Yes, Uncle,' he said, lovingly running a paw down the well-worn blade of a bat that had seen plenty of action.'

With that, the 2½-inch run machine got to his feet and walked tentatively to the wicket. Bhupathi, or Bhoo to his friends, was acknowledged as the most valuable cricket find in Dharavi for generations. His partner Viru, who had an air of confidence about him, walked over to meet him.

'Do you know who the opening bowlers are?' Bhoo asked him.

'Harsha is first up...' he motioned over to the bowler who was going through an extravagant warm up routine '...and Bogle from the other end. They are both pretty quick.'

Bhoo swallowed hard and twiddled his bat nervously.

'Come on, you like the ball coming on to the bat. It would be worse for you if they opened up with spin. I'll take the first ball, and you'll be fine. Just think of it as another game.' He made a fist and bumped gloves with Bhoo.

But it wasn't just another game, and Bhoo remembered the name Harsha. A young mouse with a fearsome reputation and the ability to vary his line and length at will.

The umpires exchanged a nod, and the one at the non-striker's end called 'Play!'

Harsha tore in and bowled, but in his excitement, he over-pitched the first ball, allowing Viru to push it into a gap for a single. Bhoo would have liked a couple more balls away from the strike and hadn't counted on being in the firing line quite so quickly.

On the boundary, Uncle crossed his fingers and muttered 'here we go' under his breath.

Out in the middle, Bhoo stuck to his usual routine. He took a guard, middle and leg, and marked it with a long scratch in the dusty wicket. He surveyed the field. Normally, he'd have been able to spot a few gaps, but today his senses seemed scrambled, the fielders a blur. He shook his head and concentrated back on his mark.

'Lots of pressure, eh?' chirped the wicketkeeper. 'The weight of all that expectation, yah. Gonna, let your whole community down, eh?' he went on.

Bhoo did his best to ignore the comments and focused on a spot on the wicket. But the unwanted 'chat' had rattled him. He became aware of his grip on the bat handle. He was holding it too tight. He needed to relax. *Take six deep breaths,* Uncle would say, but there was no time for that now.

The bowler started his approach, and Bhoo chanted a mantra in his head. *'Watch the ball, watch the ball.'* He'd say it to himself three times before the ball was delivered. Just under a second a batsman has to pick up trajectory, decide on a shot and then play it. Bhoo managed to add to this a spot of dithering and a good dollop of indecision and the ball was past him. Those there to wish him well let out an audible gasp. Up until now, he'd been oblivious to them, now there was that extra worry to further cloud his thoughts.

Viru ambled down the wicket and prodded a non-existent bump in the wicket.

'Concentrate on the next ball and forget the one that has gone before,' he suggested.

It was good advice, and having gone through his pre-delivery routine, the next ball met the middle of Bhoo's bat as he played forward solidly. A wayward ball down the leg-side followed which he met on the full, helping it to the boundary just behind square leg. Bhoo's supporters cheered up no end, and a wave of euphoria swept through him. His confidence grew and the runs came.

Mr Googly wrote in a notepad, and Uncle rubbed his chin, nodding appreciatively.

Having seen off the opening bowlers, the Mahim Junction captain brought on a leg spinner. The change from pace to spin brought some welcome relief for Bhoo. He'd need his wits about him, but with fast bowling there was always the physical threat that kept you on your toes. He'd scored 24 to date; it was a start, and he felt as though he was 'in'. He'd need to be watchful against the turning ball. There would be the odd short-pitched delivery to pick off and keep the scoreboard moving. Otherwise, he'd nudge and nurdle the ball about to accumulate rather than pile on the runs.

But if the change in pace brought a perceived let up for the batsmen, then that in itself was a dangerous thing. In truth, the change brought fresh challenges and the first ball Bhoo received from the spinner spat at him out of the dusty footmarks. The ball passed the edge of his bat as he dangled it in a speculative prod. The wicketkeeper let out an anguished howl from behind him. It suggested that things didn't get much closer to being out than that. The next ball he was more watchful. It was evident that the spinner knew what he was doing. Then a gift. The ball pitched short and wide and ideal for the cut shot. Bhoo jammed his tongue into the corner of his mouth and made to smack the ball to the boundary. Cricket is a game of small margins, a nick here, a tiny deviation there, a jag off the seam or as in this case, an edge. A bottom edge to be precise, one moment the ball was there to be hit the next the sickening sound of crashing timber behind him.

The spectators let out a collective groan, and Mr Googly shut his notebook with a snap.

'Nothing more to see here today,' he said decisively.

'What? You're going?' Uncle asked, trying to not sound too concerned.

'I am, I've seen all I need to see.'

'And what have you seen exactly?'

'A talented young man batsman certainly, but one who is impatient and headstrong. Now, can you direct me to the bus stop? I need to try and sneak on to the bus into town.'

'So does he stand a chance?'

'A chance?' Mr Googly exclaimed in mock horror. 'Based on a scrappy twenty-something, I think not.'

Uncle was horrified. It had been almost impossible to secure a scouting visit from Mr Googly. For him to leave now without seeing the best of Bhoo's batting was a disaster.

'His nerves got the better of him, that's all,' Uncle ventured.

'Nerves? I can't play a batsman who can't take a little pressure,' Mr Googly could barely conceal his astonishment.

'Don't mind please,' Uncle said, laying a paw on Mr Googly's arm. He realised that he was only making things worse.

But Mr Googly had seen Bhoo's potential, and as he turned to go, he said airily to no one in particular, 'Bring him to the basement of the Bombay Yacht Club tomorrow at 4 o'clock, I'll give him one last chance... and please, get him a decent bat.'

Bhoo trudged off the field looking downcast. Behind him, the Mahim Junction boys formed a group, shrugging their shoulders as if to say 'What now?' Uncle met him at the boundary's edge.

The relief that Mr Googly's change of heart had brought was coursing through him.

'Never mind, you did okay,' he beamed.

'Never mind? Okay? I've let the whole of Dharavi down,' said Bhoo as he pitched a well-aimed batting glove into the top of his open cricket bag.

'There are lessons to be learned, certainly, but all is not lost.' Uncle could hardly conceal his delight at the news he had to impart.

'It's no good, I can't keep a straight face any longer. You've got a second chance!'

'What? When? Where?'

'Some way from here in Colaba, you know, the 'town'. We will have to make a journey, and we'll have an errand to run on the way.'

Bhoo threw his arms round Uncle and gave him a hug.

'All right, enough of that,' Uncle snorted. 'Certain things will have to be arranged so put me down and let me get on.'

'I won't let you down... I promise,' said Bhoo before performing a pirouette of joy on one hind leg.

At the same time, eight miles high and eight hours into their nine-hour journey, the mice's travelling companion, Bonzo, woke from his induced sleep. Eight hours and 30 seconds later, he decided that his crate was not the place he wanted to be. Ten minutes of frenzied jumping, buffeting and biting bought him his freedom. No longer confined, he went on a rampage about the confined area of the hold.

The mice had settled down to sleep for the duration, but the sudden disturbance brought all three of them up to the surface. A resounding crash as a tin drum was knocked from where it had been stowed sent the mice back into their bag, leaving Bonzo to leap about the storage compartment examining the various items placed there for 'safe' transit. Eventually, he settled down with a vinyl satchel and gave the contents his undivided attention. In so doing, he proceeded to destroy the entire documentation for the contents of the hold.

The mice guiltily shrank deeper into the safety of their hiding place as the tearing, snarling noises increased. The plane had started to wobble about a bit anyway, and none of them was that keen on the sensation. The pilot had in fact started their descent into Mumbai's Chhatrapati Shivaji International Airport. Soon the full extent of Bonzo's actions would become apparent.

At the baggage carousel, there was uproar amongst those affected. A hapless airport employee was doing his best to calm them. The items that could not be accounted for had to be withheld pending emailed documentation from London. But before that, the ground crew were struggling to find someone brave enough to confront Bonzo. This was Terry Packer's problem though. For the most part the passenger's on the flight were able to make their way through the terminal. While Terry did his best to secure the release of their kit, the England players were whisked through a VIP route behind the scenes.

Morgan Smirk sneered at the gesticulating group as he wheeled his large grey suitcase through the arrivals hall. He tended to travel light to avoid such snarl-ups.

'Morgan, you are an International man of mystery, old son,' he congratulated himself on being such a seasoned globetrotter. With that in mind, the sight of a queue forming ahead made him quicken his pace. A last surge saw him slide just in front of the gentleman with the splendid hairdo and the sidekick with whom he'd had his earlier dust up. Morgan flashed a toothy grin, and the sidekick took an aggressive step towards him.

'Don't mind, don't mind,' his master restrained him in the same pleasant manner as he had before. 'We can wait.'

From the building the travellers flowed, a mixture of local people, oblivious to the commotion that absorbed them, and a more cautious element. The first time visitor, who made their way tentatively, concern etched on their faces. Into the spiced, incense-infused, heat-soaked air they trickled.

The airport's exits, VIP, First, Business or good old cattle class, fed the same car park. An excitable, enthusiastic free-for-all lay before them made up of helpers and advice givers. Everyone, it seemed, wanted to help in some capacity, and no one was shy or retiring in volunteering his services. Official porters, unofficial porters, friends of unofficial porters. There were plenty of drivers of numerous types of transport, all touting rides into the city. There were also representatives of guesthouses and small hotels clamouring for potential clients. Add to this a sizeable crowd who'd assembled on the off chance of catching a glimpse of a well-known Bollywood star who was visiting the city for the premiere of his latest film. His image stared down from a massive hoarding that overlooked the car park.

The England players were to an extent spared from this. Their team bus was located, and it eased its way through the throng and parked for them to embark. Their luggage, it had been decided, would have to follow later.

Behind them, Morgan, who was travelling on a significantly tighter budget, was left to his own resources. Although early in the morning, it was already hot, and Morgan was starting to feel it. He pushed his battered straw hat to the back of his head, puffed out his cheeks and surveyed his options. This small act marked him as a target and immediately he was inundated with offers of help. His suitcase was grabbed from one side and his laptop bag slung over his shoulder from the other. As he struggled to fight off his assailants, a loud cheer went up from the Bollywood fans. Their idol had made it out of the airport and had fleetingly appeared next to Morgan. He stood waving to his fans while his white four-by-four vehicle rolled into place. He lifted his sunglasses with one hand and smiled at the dishevelled reporter. For an instant, the billboard rising up behind him and his own supersized image framed him. Morgan waved sheepishly and was swallowed up by the Mumbai Airport masses.

Bhoo

## Chapter Five

Back in England, the disappearance of three such conspicuous members of the colony had been quickly spotted. Don had blamed himself for upsetting Compo and had been tortured by the idea that their last exchange had been a cross one.

'It was mean-spirited of me to say they couldn't go up to look at the kit bags. Particularly for Compo, he does so... *did* so love all that sort of thing,' Don reflected, his face etched with worry.

'I think that you're being a bit hard on yourself,' Mrs Heyhoe said, doing her best to raise his spirits.

'It's not my job to make the rules,' he moaned.

'Someone has to, and it isn't easy. Everybody looks up to you, and they certainly don't blame you for the boys' disappearance. It is a precarious life we lead.'

'But it wasn't an unreasonable request, was it? There again, if I could have the time again...'

'We could all say that about a lot of things.'

Ideas abounded on what had become of Compo, Beaky and Bumble. The mice knew that their existence was a hazardous one, but generally they'd managed, over the years, to limit their exposure to danger. They were pretty strict about when to venture out. Each of them highlighted hazards when they came across them—a bare electric wire, heat from a light bulb, a sharp shard of wood or an exposed nail. As long as everyone stayed alert and observant, then they'd keep the list of daily hazards to a minimum.

An old hazard that had recently been reintroduced was the attentions of Pest Arrest, the local rodent exterminators and its operatives. Their activities had been applied with renewed vigour after the appointment of Stanley, their new Head of Operations. The job had been given to him after his former colleague, Bob, had left to carve out a new career in animal preservation rather than extermination. Stanley had seized the opportunity with relish. A man on a mission, keen to employ any means, fair or foul, at his disposal, in his words to 'marmalise those mouses.'

The main headache for the mice in the 'close season' was the demolition of the old and construction of a new Warner Stand. The old stand had been built in 1958. Many of its seats provided a restricted view of the playing surface, so it had been decided that it was time for a new one. To do this, however, meant an influx of people and machinery. Work had started the day after the cricket season had ended. Taking the old structure down was a noisy business, and the little ones found that it disrupted their sleep. On the positive side, the workmen tended to be careless with their lunchtime picnics. The scavenger parties had been able to supplement the colony's rations on a daily basis with an assortment of goodies.

Then no sooner had it started than the work shuddered to a halt, and team of men in white coveralls and respirator masks replaced the demolition crew. They put up signs to keep people away from the area and roamed the site. A harmful material had been used in the construction of the old stand, and it had to be removed safely before any of the other work could proceed. This corresponded with a bout of sniffles and wheezing amongst the mouse community. The mice were convinced that the building work had somehow caused it. But on the site of the new stand, the fuss had subsided and the builders returned. The little ones seemed to be the most badly affected, and it made the adults worry.

Mrs Ranji declared that she had a recipe that would remedy the children's ailments and made a list of items that she'd need to prepare it. A bowl of barley sugar sweets, which the tour guides used to lubricate their throats, provided the main ingredient. Beefy and Thommo constructed a makeshift camp stove out of a tea light candle, and WG purloined a dessertspoon from the kitchen to boil the mixture up in. Once a sweet was melted, Mrs Ranji tossed in her secret ingredient. There was no real mystery to it, as Ranji had sourced the little beige bags of lavender for his wife from the pavilion coat check. They were intended to ward off moths, but their contents added a medicinal tang to the thick syrup.

Everyone throughout the colony was invited to have a mouthful. A large crowd formed in the communal area beneath the floorboards of the Long Room and queued for their dosage. But the act of togetherness also served to bond them as a community after their loss. A show of solidarity for those who'd lost their loved ones—Mrs Bumble, Mrs Beaky and Willow, who had a particular soft spot for Compo.

Everyone talked fondly of their friends, and the grieving wives talked of their husband's quirks.

'He was such an old worry guts,' Mrs Beaky reflected.

'...and mine could never resist a joke. Whether the time for it was appropriate or not,' Mrs Bumble said with a smile.

Willow sat away from the others, her chin resting on Compo's bat, which she held in front of her. She'd painted an emblem on it to match the new bat his favourite player in the England team used. He'd not get to use it now, but holding it made her feel close to him. Don wandered over to talk to her.

'Although we've all had our own near misses, and your own was a particularly close run thing,' Don alluded to Willow being kidnapped by the local rat population, 'it really does hit hard when one of us is actual hurt... or worse.'

The words sounded cold and harsh. He hadn't meant them to be. There really were no words that would help.

'You'll feel better, eventually, sweetie,' he concluded.

Willow gave his paw a quick squeeze and sniffed away a tear.

'Come on now, better do as the doctor, or in this case Mrs Ranji, ordered and take our medicine. Winter is just around the corner, and none of us want to get ill.'

But in truth, November had been very mild in England. The berries that fell into the Coronation Garden from the overhanging trees suggested that the local birds weren't struggling to find food. The cold weather would come in due course, and the mice would hide themselves deep inside the old pavilion.

In Mumbai, however, the heat was nudging the thermometer skyward. The England Team's bus had painstakingly threaded its way through the city's traffic. With nearly two million road users and not enough road to go around, progress had been slow. Outside the bus, the Mumbaiker drivers played a game to local rules, jumping traffic signals, overtaking on the wrong side and cutting across lanes whilst incessantly honking their horns. For the players, it was better to let someone else worry about it, and for the most part, they tuned it out or catnapped.

Most of them had been to India before, whether touring with England parties or playing in the Indian Premier League. For those accustomed to international travel, there was little thrill in airports and the to-ing and fro-ing between them. But even for these seasoned travellers, arriving in the unofficial tourist zone of Colaba, they couldn't help but be struck by the familiarity of some of the local architecture.

In the old British Quarter, they rounded the Regal Cinema circle, or roundabout, with its 1933 movie theatre, a white-plastered, art deco building that wouldn't look out of place in any city in the UK. Then past the Bombay Yacht Club, a large colonial building whose glory was somewhat faded but still had an air of grandeur with a magical collection of staggered pitched roofs and conical topped turrets. The architect had combined both mock Tudor beams and Mughal arched windows in, what one might call, a 'Hogwarts style'. From its prime position on the harbour, it overlooked Mumbai's great landmark, the Gateway of India—a great ceremonial arch built to commemorate the visit of King George V in 1911, but not actually finished until 1924. Tourists crowded the area and were doing their best to ward off the attentions of various hawkers, photographers, snake charmers and 'hangers-on'. As they did so, just beside them, the England Team coach pulled up outside one of the city's most splendid hotels.

Unbeknownst to the team, their belongings were still being ferried to them. When the team's luggage had eventually made it out of the airport, there had been no transportation for it. There had been many offers from willing volunteers of help, all of them politely declined by Terry the kit man. He'd shown his resourcefulness by convincing a cricket-loving policeman to commandeer a double decker bus to ferry the bags. In a 'follow that team bus' scenario, the bus driver had made an excellent job of throwing his enormous vehicle around the constricted roads of the Mumbai Metropolitan Region. In fact, his road handling was so vigorous that eventually his three furry hitchhikers stuck their heads out to see what was going on. By the look of Terry, who was hanging on for dear life, they were better off 'down below'. A squeal of rubber on tarmac as they rounded a corner confirmed this and sent them scurrying back into the layers of padding and clothing.

Before long, the bus made it to Colaba and drew up outside the team's hotel. Now stationary, it was as if the vehicle was left panting after its exertions; it reeked of oil and burnt rubber. The radiator sizzled and its cap threatened to blow. Despite the danger, an army of hotel porters swarmed down the steps of the hotel and over the bus, stripping it of its baggage. After his ordeal, Terry made his way unsteadily up the steps to the hotel foyer, where a debonair young man glided over to meet him.

'I'm sorry for your trouble, sir.' He motioned to an assistant, who stepped forward and draped a garland of flowers around his neck. Followed by another, who approached and dabbed an ochre Tilak mark on his forehead. 'Here is a list of the players' rooms,' he concluded with a deep bow.

Together, he and Terry sorted through the luggage. As they were located, the players' personal bags were despatched to their rooms in the hotel elevators while the kit bags were placed on hotel luggage carts and rolled off in another direction.

As they were pushed across the foyer, Mr Gogi Singh, manager of the hotel bookshop, was making his way to work. He'd arrived, as usual, on his 'pop wheel' as he called it, a dilapidated scooter that he parked at a friend's shop behind the hotel. He liked the convenience of his 'pop wheel', but as a cautious creature, he was caught in a quandary of crash helmet wearing or turban wearing. He'd got round this to some extent by wearing a builder's hardhat on top of his turban with a long chinstrap. This, however, really meant that he was only protected from things falling from above rather than it saving him should he fall off, but it eased his conscience. It did, nonetheless, mean that he had to suffer the unwanted attentions of those of the local scallywag fraternity, who delighted in poking fun at him every morning.

The bookshop seemed out of place in the swanky hotel. A curious dark and dusty corner lined with black-painted shelves and stocked floor to ceiling with books. Gogi prided himself on his extensive stock, which ranged from antique copies to splendid 'coffee table books' or the latest releases. He'd take a book back too, as the odd well-thumbed second-hand tome suggested. The locally printed and so discounted books were a delight to visiting bookworms. He also did a roaring trade in a great stock of local handicraft cards and stationery. Not forgetting his complimentary bookmarks that were presented to every customer with a flourish, each printed with the strapline 'Don't say goodbye to Mumbai without a good buy at Gogi's'. It wasn't going to win any caption competitions, but he liked the alliteration, and they were nicely embellished with a paisley design.

Gogi unlocked the shutter to the shop and bent down to retrieve a bundle of letters that had been wedged under it. Inside the shop, he undid the frayed string that bound them and leafed through the pile. A bill, a circular and a crisp white formal-looking envelope stamped with an emblem that formed the letters 'CCI'.

'Hmm, what do we have here?' he mused as he ran a finger under the gummed flap. He slipped an impressive-looking card from the envelope and read.

*The Cricket Club of India requests the pleasure of your company at a cricket match to commemorate the centenary of the Bombay Brothers' 1915 Cricket Match between an Invitational XI and the England Touring side.*

'Well I never,' Gogi said to himself.

'Well you never what?' asked his assistant Rajesh, who'd just entered the shop carrying two small clay cups of chai tea.

'See for yourself,' said Gogi, swapping the invitation card for one of the small cups, which he drained with a slurp.

'Oooh, that's very grand. Why should they ask you?' Rajesh asked in a tone that Gogi thought was rather disrespectful.

'Why shouldn't they ask me? I'm from a very noble family, I'll have you know.'

'Yes, of course, excuse me,' Rajesh stuttered, remembering that his livelihood relied upon Gogi. 'But there must be a special reason that you've been invited.'

'My Great Grandfather Bilal played in a special cricket match in the First World War. He told me about it once when I was a little boy. He was a big, burly fellow and was a pretty pacey fast bowler I believe.'

'Ah, so it looks as though you've been invited to this centenary match because you're related to one of the original participants,' Rajesh observed while re-examining the invitation.

'That would appear to be the case,' said Gogi, taking the card off his assistant. He slid it under the cash register for safekeeping. He then barked orders at Rajesh to tidy up the shop in readiness for the first customers of the day.

Across the hotel lobby, the mice were aware that the narrative of sound that had accompanied their recent travels had quietened down somewhat. A cacophony of traffic noise and horn blowing had been replaced by the sedate twinkling of a grand piano. This incongruous accompaniment to the Indian setting was provided by the French import of Gaston Le Pew, the pianist. For him, wearing a fixed smile and a tuxedo at any time of day was an occupational hazard that went with the job. As he picked out an extravagant re-working of the theme to the film 'Titanic', the mice had a team meeting.

'Brrr... it's suddenly got cold in here,' shivered Beaky.

'I'm going up top to see what's going on,' said Bumble.

'Let's all go together,' Compo cautioned. 'We're a long way from home, and whatever happens, happens to us all.'

Together, the three friends scrabbled up through the bag's contents. They squeezed their heads out of the gap in the zip just as Gaston, with an ostentatious wave of his hand, finished a tumultuous passage of the piece he was playing. The mice were partway through their journey of being wheeled across the reception area on their way to the service elevators. As they passed Gaston, their eyes met his, and for a moment, his faultless smile slipped and froze into a horrific mask of consternation. Had he really seen three mice in a neat row checking in to the hotel? He momentarily lost his place and the music faltered.

The manager of the hotel was making his rounds, and he brought Monsieur Gaston back to his senses with a loud 'AHEM!'

In that instant, the luggage cart passed out of sight and behind the scenes on its journey into the hotel's inner workings.

The elevator door closed behind them with a swish and a clunk, and then the cabin shuddered into action with a whirr of its motor.

'Going down, I think,' said Bumble.

But no sooner had their descent begun than it came to abrupt halt. The elevator door slid open and two houseboys unceremoniously unloaded the bags. They clearly hadn't undergone the same baggage-handling course as the front line staff.

Inside their kit bag, the mice were jolted, bashed and crushed until their bag came to rest along with the others. Pushed up against a wall, the bags snaked their way along a corridor. For a while, the mice sat tight and listened. Somebody walked past wearing squeaky-soled shoes. A distant door banged, and then silence.

Once again, the three furry travellers ventured out. The featureless corridor stretched away from them in both directions.

'What do we do now?' Beaky asked, bleakly breaking the silence.

'That, my good fellow, remains to be seen,' Bumble exclaimed brightly, trying to lighten the mood.

'We can stay put and see where we're taken to next,' Beaky suggested.

'Chances are that the kit will stay here until the players need it for practice. In that case, we could be here for a day or two. I don't know about you, but I'm definitely going to need something to eat before then,' Compo said, being practical.

'I'd rather be hungry and safe,' Beaky moaned.

'All right, you stay safe and we'll go. Come on, Bumble.'

'Wait a moment, I'm not sure I'm volunteering,' Bumble said, his voice faltering.

'What? You're not going to let me down too, Bumble, are you?'

'No, but...'

His excuse was interrupted by something speeding towards and then past them. The heads of the three mice swung from left to right in unison as if they were watching the ball in a tennis match.

'Did you see what I saw?' Bumble asked.

'If you're saying, did I just see a mouse ride past on a three-wheeled bicycle... then, yes,' Compo replied, his response tinged with disbelief.

Beaky, it seemed, was speechless until he announced, 'Hang on, he's coming back.'

'Quick, follow me!' Compo cried. And with that, he launched himself from the top of the kit bag.

'Geronimo!' cried Bumble and followed him.

'Oh heck!' wailed Beaky and followed suit.

The three friends got to their feet and made a makeshift roadblock by linking arms. Bumble held up a paw as if he was a policeman. The bicycle-riding mouse pedalled furiously towards them, head down.

'He isn't going to see us,' warned Beaky.

'Don't worry, he'll see us,' Compo insisted.

'Oooerr... no, he isn't. Scarper!' yelled Bumble.

Bumble and Beaky ran in opposite directions, leaving Compo. Normally he was so decisive, but he hesitated, and in the end, froze.

At the same time, the cyclist, who'd been struggling with his machine, looked up. To his horror, suddenly there was a pedestrian where before there had been no one. He pulled hard on the handlebars in order to avoid him. Compo put his paws over his eyes, and the three-wheeler veered away. As it did so, one of its wheels left the ground, and the unstable vehicle toppled and slid across the corridor. From it spilled its precious cargo of 'Golden Gateway' finest basmati rice. For an instant, the bike's rider was down, but he was on in feet in no time. It was obvious whom he felt was to blame for the accident, and he raced over to Compo.

'What do you think you are doing? Trying to do away with me, are you?' he shouted at Compo.

Beaky and Bumble had scurried over and arrived slightly breathless.

'Now hang on a minute, son, it was an accident, that's all,' Bumble said, trying to defuse the situation.

'Look at my rickshaw, look at my supplies!' the driver moaned.

'We'll help get you sorted,' Bumble continued to try and calm him.

'Will you two stop it?' Beaky called over to them. 'I think Compo's in shock.'

They all gathered around Compo, who was shaking and not looking well at all. Bumble put a comforting arm round him.

'Poor thing. We've all had a pretty eventful day and night and are a long way from home. I guess the scare just tipped him over the edge.'

'If that is the case, come on, help me get my rickshaw up, and we'll take him to my home.'

Beaky and the rickshaw's driver scampered over to the three-wheeler. It was a bit of a struggle, but the two mice righted it and pushed it into position. Behind the saddle was a bench seat set over the back wheels.

'Come on, Compo, let's get you up. This kind gent is going to give you a ride,' Bumble urged his friend gently.

'Sunni!' the bicycling mouse responded.

'Oh yes, it's bloomin' hot here, you're right there,' Bumble replied, slightly puzzled at this sudden reference to the weather.

'No, my name is Sunni.'

'Oh, I see. Well, this here's Beaky, the patient is Compo, and I'm Bumble. How do you do?'

Together, the three mice lifted Compo onto the bicycle rickshaw, and Bumble and Beaky climbed onto to the seat either side of him. Sunni then swung his back leg over the cycle part of the contraption.

'Hold on tight, everybody!' he called over his shoulder.

'Wait, Compo's cap! He never goes anywhere without his cap,' cried Beaky.

'I'll get it,' said Sunni, skipping off the rickshaw and retrieving Compo's faded blue cap. He held it in his paws and examined it for a moment.

'This is a cricket cap,' he observed.

'It is indeed,' replied Bumble. 'All the way from Lord's Cricket Ground in London, where we live.'

'Not *the* Lord's.'

'Yup!'

'I don't believe it,' said Sunni.

'Well, we're not asking you to, but it's the truth. We stowed away, by accident, in England cricket team's kit and now here we are... err, where are we exactly?'

'Mumbai... India!' beamed Sunni.

'I kinda gathered that,' grinned Bumble.

'You're in the basement of one of the city's finest hotels. I was just helping myself to some of the kitchen supplies when I ran into you,' Sunni chuckled, now able to see the funny side. 'When I say 'finest' I mean '*FINE-EST*,' he emphasised the word. 'There aren't many places that the likes of me can get his paws on the speciality of Golden Gateway triple A-grade basmati rice. Mmm-hmmm.'

'In that case, shouldn't we pick it up?' suggested Beaky.

'No, don't worry, I can always come back later and get some more. Anyway, it is good to occasionally leave some evidence of mouse activity because then the chef thinks we live here.

But that's what we want him to think. He gets the Mouse Killer people to go to all sorts of trouble to get rid of us from here while we're safely somewhere else.'

'So you don't live in the hotel?' asked Bumble.

'No. I live somewhere far more extraordinary, and I think that given where you say you live, you're going to find it interesting.'

'Why's that?' croaked Compo, who'd been listening and had started to perk up.

'Because I live at the centre of the mouse cricketing world.'

'And where might that be?' asked Bumble sceptically.

'The Bombay Yacht Club?'

'The Bombay *What* Club?' Bumble spluttered in disbelief.

'Hang on tight, I'll show you,' and with that, Sunni pedalled his passengers off down the corridor as fast as he could.

Bashar

## Chapter Six

Bhoo and Uncle had quite a day ahead of them. They'd set off early having said their goodbyes the night before. Bhoo's Amma had made them both a snack for the journey, and Uncle had stowed it in a backpack that he'd slung over one shoulder. They'd slipped out of Dharavi before dawn after Uncle had given Bhoo a final inspirational speech before they left home.

'This day will bring with it many challenges. There will be times when you are in danger and times when you are afraid. Your body may cry out for a rest, and your mind may become overloaded with the pressures you have to endure.'

Bhoo looked at Uncle wide eyed and swallowed hard.

'Don't worry; I will be there by your side at all times. When in doubt, remember the saying "This is not a game we are playing for fun and entertainment. This is a fight we must win."'

'Is that an ancient Indian proverb?' Bhoo asked.

'No, it is a line from my favourite Bollywood cricket movie *Lagaan!*'

With that, Uncle had clapped his protégé on the back and pushed him into the street. At that hour, the street dogs and cats, which might make their journey risky, were still in whatever bed they'd found for the night. However, an early start is not something unique to little cricketers and their mentors in Mumbai. Along their route, yellow electric light glowed through thin curtains or spilled out from under ill-fitting doors as the city came to life. So they scurried and hopped and bounded their way from a shadow here to the cover of a weed there. They ducked behind a discarded can or flattened themselves under a piece of newspaper. It was tricky, but their progress was swift and unimpeded.

They made their way to Mahim Junction. It was more an extended village than a railway station. It had generated a community that crept farther down the line on an almost daily basis. Whether its residents, who lived by the rails, liked it or not, trains bringing in the junction's share of Mumbai's daily seven million passengers had already started to arrive. To handle that weight of numbers, things need to start early. As the rush hour approached, further trains would soon be arriving with carriages overstuffed to bursting. The authorities even have an official term for it—a Super Dense Crush Load.

Having squeezed through the perimeter fence, the mice skipped along through makeshift dwellings. Inside, their inhabitants got ready for their day as the mice scampered by. But the impromptu settlement brought with it the debris of modern life and the trackside was strewn with litter. For the Municipal Corporation to keep on top of it was a thankless and never-ending task. For the mice, it provided them with the cover they needed to make it to the junction's main building. It was a hazardous journey, but the nice needn't have worried. Everyone was far too busy concentrating on their ablutions and breakfasts to take issue with a couple of mice scampering by.

They passed between two legs protruding from a blue-checked lungi. The legs' owner was brushing his teeth up above them. He swung a poorly aimed kick at them as they passed, stubbing his toe in the process. But as he hopped about nursing his big toe, the mice ran on. After all, a couple of scrawny rodents were hardly an uncommon sight in the litter-strewn surroundings.

Uncle had planned the route meticulously. It would take patience, timing and good fortune, but if all the pieces came together, they'd make it to their destination and do a spot of shopping on the way. Their gateway to the means of achieving this was the vending machine in the station ticket office. From here, the pair could wait for their ride with a panoramic view through the glass and a ready supply of snacks.

The ticket clerk's window, opposite the machine, was on this morning occupied by the Assistant Station Master Moti Kumar. He'd had two calls from staff members crying off sick that morning, and as a result had to man the ticket desk himself. He'd had a busy morning with a queue of impatient would-be travellers snaking round the ticket hall. He'd hoped for a little time to himself, as he'd received an interesting-looking envelope through the mail. As something of a cricket fanatic, he'd recognised the Cricket Club of India emblem and was intrigued as to why they were contacting him.

By midmorning, the queue had started to thin out. Moti decided to award himself a break. Just as he made to leave his desk, his local dabbawala, Suresh Chaskar arrived.

'Morning sir. I have your tiffin box for you.'

Suresh was a part of the amazing delivery system of around 4,000 dabbawalas across Mumbai. Every day, 160,000 home-cooked lunches from the kitchens of wives and mothers are delivered direct to Mumbai's workers. The key to how Suresh helped work this magic was his heavy-framed bicycle. He'd propped it against the building, its handlebars and rear carrier slung with the tiffin boxes of his other clients.

Suresh's appearance was the cue for the mice to leave their hiding place and make sure they were on his bike before he set off again.

'Right, here we go, Bhoo. Follow me,' instructed Uncle, who'd been keeping an eye open for the dabbawala. He leapt from his perch and landed in the vending machine's chute that dispensed the snacks. It had a nice polished curve, and it launched him on his way. He left the machine in a neat arc and hit the floor of the ticket hall running. Bhoo was hard on his heels.

Once at the bicycle, Uncle made it onto the tiffin boxes attached to the carrier with a jump that belied his age. He set himself and looked for Bhoo in order to give him a helping hand. It was a freak accident, but Uncle was horrified to find that the young mouse had been halted by the boot heel of a policeman doing his rounds. Trapped by the tail, Bhoo squirmed about in an effort to free himself. Uncle urged him frantically, but he was powerless. Then, when all seemed lost, the policeman made an about turn and meandered off. Bhoo didn't hesitate and ran the short distance, catching Uncle's outstretched arms to haul himself to safety.

The dabbawala returned and mounted his trusty velocipede, setting off for his next client. As the mice clung to the top of one the clanking tiffin boxes, Uncle put a reassuring arm round his young charge.

'I never said we wouldn't have a hiccup.'

The mice sat tight as their unofficial chauffeur completed his rounds, re-adjusting their perch as required as he delivered the lunches in his care to their owners. However, their patience paid off, and eventually they arrived at their first destination, Crawford Market. Here, despite the frenzied activity above ground around the old market buildings, was housed an underground emporium known to just a few. With its entrance under an old iron boot scraper set into the wall of the Victorian façade, 'Bombay Bats R Us' was a well-kept secret. Its master bat maker, AJ, normally took work in or made bats to order. However, a select few, or those in the know, might get the complete personalised service if they should stop by.

Suresh unhooked four more boxes from the handlebars. With an average of five minutes a delivery, this gave the mice just enough time to conclude their business. They dropped from the back of the bicycle and nipped through the ancient iron arch of the boot scraper. The arch was inscribed in tiny letters 'Bats R Us – Purveyors of the world's smallest cricket bats.'

'HELLO! Is there anybody home?' Uncle called out.

'Oh my goodness, I recognise the sound of that old reprobate!' came the response from within.

Bhoo and Uncle found AJ in a cluttered workshop surrounded by cricket bats in various states of manufacture and repair. The two old friends hugged each other in greeting.

'I must introduce you to my latest, and I must say, perhaps brightest young prospect,' Uncle burst out enthusiastically.

'Oh yes, you've had a few of those in your time,' AJ said with a wry look.

'Precisely, this boy is going to need all the help he can get! Once he's armed with one of your 'railway sleepers', err... I mean beautifully crafted precision blades, then we'll be on to something.'

'Hmm...' AJ twiddled the end of his upturned waxed moustache thoughtfully. 'So how much were you thinking of spending?'

'Ahh, now we have a bit of a problem there,' Uncle stuttered. 'I was wondering if you would like to be his sponsor.'

'Okay, thank you, I've heard enough... goodbye,' AJ barked, pushing his friend gently but firmly out of his workshop.

'No wait, listen.' Uncle proceeded to tell AJ the story of Bhoo's unsuccessful trial and the fact that in spite of that, Mr Googly had given him a second chance.

'Googly sees his talent too, don't you see?'

'I'll give you that, Googly knows his stuff.'

'So may we have a bat, please Mr AJ... sir?' Uncle put his hands together in prayer.

'Very well, but a practice bat only.'

'No, no, no... a match bat... and the best you have!'

'You're pushing your luck, my friend.'

'Come now, you know you want to really. Here, Bhoo, come and try a few.'

Bhoo had kept out of the negotiations, and he stepped forward tentatively. Uncle was now in full flow.

'He needs a bat with a light pick up but plenty of meat in the middle.'

'Ignore this old fool,' AJ advised, motioning to Bhoo to join him. 'Come with me, young mouse. I may have just the right blade for you.'

Uncle made to join them.

'Give us a moment, Uncle. I need to see if he can handle just what I have in mind for him,' AJ instructed mysteriously.

In no time, a bat had been selected and Uncle and Bhoo took their leave of AJ, making their way back to their ride. They found Suresh, the dabbawala, remonstrating with the owner of the railings to which his bike was padlocked. In a city where all sorts of rules are being broken at any time of the day, it seemed a trifle picky. However, it gave the mice a little extra time to scrabble back up amongst the tiffin boxes. One of them was hung in a nice blue and white checked bag. It belonged to Filippo, the shirt maker, and the mice made a beeline for it. Here they were able to snuggle down out of sight and wait while Suresh pedalled them to their ultimate destination.

Compo, Beaky and Bumble were just arriving at that same destination.

'Not much farther, guys,' Sunni puffed as he danced on the pedals of the rickshaw.

It had been quite a ride on Sunni's rickety machine. He'd explained that he had acquired it from a shop at Chor Bazaar, a well-known flea market that sold second-hand, antique and vintage items. The rickshaw had been a children's toy. It was difficult to determine how old it was, but if wonkiness was anything to go by, it was more antique than second-hand.

They'd eased off to start with, Sunni straining with the extra weight, but once he'd got the machine rolling, they'd started to make good headway along the corridor in the hotel's basement.

As the passengers started to get used to the motion of the machine, Sunni unexpectedly veered off the straight. A flick of the handlebars, a bump and they left the building down a long forgotten pipe. Instantly they were plunged into darkness with just a dot of light ahead of them.

Sunni had pedalled on regardless, having completed the journey on a regular basis. For his passengers, it was a ride they were worried was never going to end.

'Ay up,' Bumble exclaimed in his broad Lancashire accent. 'I do believe that dot is getting bigger.'

He was right, and the mice were nearing the end of their journey. Suddenly they burst into the light. As they squinted to accustom themselves to the transition, they tried to make sense of what they could see. They appeared to be teetering on the brink of a precipice, but when they looked harder, they realised they were overlooking a magnificent tubular amphitheatre. Ordered and carefully laid out. Then the noise broke through, a cacophony of high-pitched squeaks.

'What is this?' said Compo, wide-eyed. Bumble and Beaky stared dumbly at the scene before them.

'Swagat hai. Welcome, to the centre of the cricket universe,' Sunni exclaimed with a twist of an outstretched forepaw. 'This is the BYC Cricketarium. A residence and stadium all in one.'

'But how...?' Beaky trailed off, still lost for words.

'It is the old wine cellar for the Bombay Yacht Club above us. You see, the bays for the wine bottles are arranged in a nice spiral that overlooks our cricket ground.'

'And in each one is a family of mice?' suggested Compo.

'We like to cram in a few more than one, but, yes.'

'It's very bright. I'm not sure I'd get much shut-eye if I lived here,' Bumble said grumpily.

'Our indoor sun is the secret of our success, and we have learned to live with it. It is particularly useful for day/night games. It is only when it goes out that we have a problem. Then we have to make some sort of commotion so that the people have to investigate what is happening. Someone comes crashing about in the dark. The children get all frightened, everyone hides, and we wait while the light bulb gets changed.'

'Very clever, much like our life at Lord's; you learn to live on your wits,' Compo smiled. But as he thought of home, which suddenly felt very distant, he felt a tear in his eye and turned away.

'You must be exhausted,' Sunni changed the subject. 'Let's find you something to eat and a place to rest.'

He wheeled his rickshaw into a recess scraped out of the plaster walls and motioned for the three English mice follow him.

'We have to walk all the way round to the other side to get the elevator down.'

'I'm glad to hear that,' Beaky spluttered. 'I do not like the look of those stairs, or rather what's left of those stairs.'

A wooden spiral staircase had once served the cylindrical wine cellar, but it had long since been out of commission, and now only the first four steps remained. Compo and Bumble edged over, had a tentative look over the side and then quickly fell into step behind Sunni.

The lift was a simple construction of a boxcar attached by a rope to an axle that ran through a pulley wheel. The device depended on the services of a volunteer who cranked a handle at one end of the axle. This lowered or lifted the basket to order.

A couple of streets away, Bhoo and Uncle had arrived at Filippo the Shirt makers' shop and left their ride. The shop was right next to the side entrance of the Bombay Yacht Club. They'd just have to give the doorman the slip. He was soon distracted. A portly gentleman had arrived by one of the city's compact black and yellow taxis and was struggling to get out of it. While he was occupied in helping with the extraction, the mice made their move. Bhoo's cricket bat impeded their progress a bit, but they pushed, shoved, hauled and scrambled up the five steps and disappeared into the elderly building.

'Wait, a second,' puffed Uncle. 'Just let me catch my breath, then we'll make our way down to the cellar.'

The two mice huddled behind the club umbrella stand while the older of the two mopped his brow. He'd made the journey on numerous occasions due to his links with the mouse cricketing fraternity, but he was aware that he wasn't getting any younger and that soon his involvement in the game would be solely as a spectator. Bhoo took the opportunity to examine his new bat.

'I love the smell of my bat,' cooed Bhoo, clearly thrilled with his acquisition.

'Hmm, there's nothing quite like the smell of linseed oil on willow,' Uncle agreed. 'I'd have thought AJ could have found something a little better. It looks as though it has had quite a battering. However, a bat from AJ is a special thing, so you had better take care of it and make sure that any more marks on it are just cherries from the ball. Here, wrap my *pheta* around it.' He handed his young charge his colourful headscarf.

In the late 1800s a style of building had developed in the city. Think of the Houses of Parliament blended with traditional Indian features. Indian architects embraced this Victorian Bombay Gothic style, and they created structures of thick stonewalls, wonderful patterned stone inlay floors and high ceilings. But the maintenance of such buildings was costly and impractical. This could only make the mice's journey easier.

With the precious bat secure, they slipped behind the faded glory of the buildings décor and into its fabric. Slipping through a network of floorboards, hollow walls and ancient plumbing, they descended to the basement and squeezed themselves out of a hole in the plaster.

They emerged, dusted themselves down and found themselves in a cell sealed by a high arched, ancient door. In the floor was a large wooden disc. A shaft of light shone from a knothole long since punched out near its edge. Uncle scampered over to it, and without hesitating, he dropped through it and out of sight. For a moment Bhoo paused at the opening.

'Pass your bat down and follow me,' Uncle called.

The young mouse fed the precious bat through and then followed it.

The mice waiting for the elevator had already 'fielded' Uncle as he dropped to the ground, so they were ready to catch the owner of the furry bottom and scrabbling legs who'd followed him down.

'I hope you guys can cope with the arrival all these new faces.' Compo made a gesture to take in the group.

'Don't you worry. I know this old fellow.' Sunni clapped Uncle round the back. 'In any case, we'll be expecting many more visitors for tomorrow's trial match.'

'That is indeed why we're here,' Uncle acknowledged. 'This is my young protégé Bhoo,' he introduced the young mouse to the group.

'How do you do?' Compo replied. 'This is Beaky and that's Bumble. We're from England.'

'I see you have the England cricket cap.' Uncle pointed to Compo's faded cap and wrinkled his nose.

'What, this old thing?' Compo patted his head. 'I wouldn't go anywhere without it.'

'What have you got there, young'un?' Bumble asked Bhoo, cheerfully changing the subject and bringing him into the conversation.

'My new bat, sir.'

'Sir?' Bumble spluttered. 'Nobody's ever called me 'sir' before, but I dare say I could grow to like it. Bring it over and let's 'ave a look.'

Bhoo unwrapped his bat held it out proudly for Bumble to inspect.

'When you said "new", I thought you meant 'new'. This old thing has seen plenty of action.'

'New to me, sir,' Bhoo replied defensively.

'V-V-S,' Bumble read off the top of the bat just below the handle.

'Very-Very-Special,' Uncle butted in. 'From the finest bat maker in Mumbai.'

Just then the elevator arrived, much to the relief of Compo and Beaky.

'Shall we?' Compo suggested, and they all crammed into it.

'Let her go, Ishy,' Sunni called out to the lanky mouse who manned the handle. Ishy responded with a mock salute and gently lowered the elevator car.

Slowly they descended to the bottom of the old cylindrical wine cellar. The old wine bays had been turned into dormitories housing more than one family.

'The lift must get very busy, Sunni,' Compo observed as they descended past the dwellings that spiralled down, each stacked one on top of the other.

'The individual bays have all been connected with clay ramps built over the years. If you're fit enough and don't get too giddy, you could wind your way all the down to the bottom on foot.'

'So I guess the whole place relies on everyone getting along.'

'Everyone is pretty cool about sharing space—this is India, everywhere is crowded!'

They arrived at the bottom with a slight jolt and stepped out. Before them stretched the broad green expanse of the BYC Cricketarium Ground (courtesy of the club's Billiard table renovation.) It was quite unlike anything the three residents of the Lord's Pavilion had ever seen.

Ayesha

**Chapter Seven**

Moti Kumar's whole routine revolved around an early start. It suited his approach to life—to get up early, have a full day and then go to bed dog-tired. Unfortunately, he'd been so excited, having opened his invitation to the Centenary Game from the Cricket Club of India, that he'd been unable to get to sleep. Calling all his friends and relations on his 'handy', or mobile, phone that evening hadn't helped. He was convinced that he now had a permanent buzz in his head from over using it. In fact, the buzzing was coming from a transformer mounted on a pole outside his home by the local electric company.

He was woken with a jolt by his alarm clock at 4.30 AM. He'd staggered bleary eyed from his bed to the bathroom. The buzz in his head seemed worse than ever. Later that day, a technician from the electric company would adjust it, leaving him to believe that the phone had indeed caused it. As a result, he'd treat his handset with the utmost suspicion for the next few days.

He sat down to a breakfast of a sad dry roti and a banana while he listened to the radio. The presenter was annoyingly chirpy given the anti-social hour.

'So the England Currrr-icket team is in town and it's time to PART-AY!' the presenter brayed.

Moti decided it was time to change the station, but the next announcement made him hesitate.

'This weekend at the Cricket Club of India, a chance to see these guys as you've never seen them before, up close and personal in a charity game. More of that in a moment after this top tune for you cricket lovers out there. It's 'Chokra', which some of you might remember as the theme music of the 1996 World Cup.'

As the east meets west fusion pop song faded out, the disc jockey continued.

'So get down to the Cricket Club of India this weekend for a commemorative match. Help celebrate one hundred years since a great act of brotherhood during the First World War. Listeners, let's get out and support this event. It's a great cause, raising funds and awareness for retired servicemen.'

The disc jockey played a sound effect of a cricket bat hitting a ball followed by the roar of a crowd. 'Tock!..... RAAAAAAA!'

'Yes indeed, people, The England cricket team against a team of past greats in your hometown, MUMBAI!' More canned roaring followed. 'To get you more in the mood, a tune, no delete that... an anthem that whenever you hear it just screams CRICKET.' The *sound of the BBC's cricket coverage, 'Soul Limbo.'*

The BBC's Test Match Special theme tune played over the airwaves. Even as a cricket lover, Moti felt he couldn't take much more. But at the end of the track, the presenter continued.

'I don't know about you guys, but the bit I like about a cricket competition is when one team gets the trophy. You know what I mean? Ticker tape, everyone does a lap of honour, the man of the hour gets carried shoulder high. What's not to like? For this game, it's about the taking part and remembering our heroic brothers from the past. But hey, Mumbai, I'm putting it out there. There must be someone, somewhere who'd like to make a presentation. So my message is... "jaldi chalo", text it to your friends, share it on social networks, "Come on get going", let's find this game a prize.'

Moti turned the radio off with a dig of his finger on the on/off button. He'd had enough of the DJ, and in any case, he had to get to work. The cricket match was obviously going to be a big deal, and he was proud to have his own very special invitation to the game. He closed his front door with a bang that caused a light sprinkling of dust to fall from its frame. The meagre dwelling was left in silence aside from the annoying buzz of a tuk tuk horn passing by outside. On the wall to the side of the door hung a faded black and white photograph. A young man with a patchy moustache stared out of it into the room. His crumpled baggy battledress suggested hardship and weight-loss. His boots muddied from the trenches. His lightly tanned features were a mix of Europe and the Subcontinent beneath a battered cap. The man in the picture was Sanjeev Kumar, Private soldier and member of the 1914 Indian Expeditionary Force to France and the reason for Moti's invitation to the Centenary Game.

Back in London, the Lord's night-watchman Gary Nicholls was having trouble with his TV. Sid Pickett, who manned the little cabin during the day, had re-tuned it to the Sci-Fi Channel and since then the remote had developed a mind of its own. Eventually, he managed to get the infrared signal to register by going outside the cabin and firing it back in through the window. In the dark of the London night, the brightly sunlit ground of the Hagley Oval in New Zealand beamed from the screen. Back inside, Gary rubbed his hands in glee and settled down to a night of test cricket 'down under'. He grabbed a large bag of crisps and began to munch on them noisily. Beside him on top of the bank of closed circuit televisions that monitored the ground sat a line of relieved visitors.

Don, Mikey, Gatt, Fred, WG and Beefy had all congregated for the televised match.

'Thank goodness for that,' whispered Beefy, whose idea it had been to watch the game. He'd stumbled upon the coverage of the first day's play on an expedition and had badgered the others to join him. Some of them had been wary about venturing out so far. However, with the gloom of the disappearance of their friends still hanging over the colony, any distraction was welcome.

'Compo would have loved this,' Fred mumbled sadly.

'It does look lovely and sunny,' WG sighed as the camera panned round the grassy slopes of supporters watching the game.

'And all those picnics,' Gatt added. 'It looks pretty good to me. Perhaps that's what happened to the others. They decided to go on holiday. Somewhere nice and hot.'

'You've got to be jokin', man,' Mikey snapped. 'Don't say things that are just plain daft.'

'Shhhh,' Don reprimanded him, partly to change the subject and partly to make sure they weren't detected. A misplaced squeak might give them away. Having made the effort to get there, they might as well get their money's worth so to speak.

Gary finished his crisps, crumpled the bag and tossed it basketball style towards the waste bin. A hush descended on the cabin, punctuated by the sound of ball on willow and the observations of the commentator. From their lofty vantage point, the friends sat in a line, their faces illuminated by the glow of the screen, enjoying a glimpse of summer and remembering days spent watching cricket with Compo, Beaky and Bumble.

## Chapter Eight

The three Londoners had been billeted in a shelter similar to a dugout at a baseball or football field. It was hardly five star, but after their adventures, they slept long and soundly. Bhoo and Uncle had snuggled up at one end of it as well.

As a result, they were all woken when 'Woolly', the head coach and groundsman of the BYC Cricketarium, started barking orders. He, in association with Mr Googly, would be making the selection for Bombay Yacht Club (Mouse XI) for their next match. It was against their rivals, the Mumbai Cricketeers Invitational XI. It was a must win game for the prestigious area title and a splendid cup, of which the Cricketeers were the holders. Woolly, who was so named because he wore a woolly bobble hat, whatever the weather, was doing his rounds. As the mice got themselves up, it was apparent that it was going to be a busy day. On the pitch in front of them, a number of mice had drifted in with assorted pieces of cricketing paraphernalia.

'Morning, sleep well?' Sunni greeted them all brightly. 'Come and have some breakfast.'

'Look sharp now, boy,' Uncle said in a gruff morning voice to Bhoo, who was finding it hard to wake up.

Sunni led the sleepy group to a rickety shelter from which a well-fed character was serving small filled buns. Judging by the queue, either everyone was very hungry or what he was serving was very popular.

'Whatever he's cooking smells pretty good,' Beaky cooed, sniffing the air.

'Well, with your magnificent nose, don't mind please, you are well qualified to judge,' Sunni replied with a smile.

Beaky opened his mouth to protest.

'He's not called Beaky for nothing,' Compo butted in. 'So what is it that we can smell?'

'Vada pav—a sort of potato sandwich.'

'Potato? Uggh horrible lumpy things,' spluttered Bumble, despite the fact that just at that moment his tummy made a loud rumbling sound.

'I am thinking that you will be liking Ramesh's cooking, and Ramesh and famish sound pretty good together, no?' Sunni joked, at which they all laughed.

The queue edged forwards, and just as the friends got to the front of it, an athletically built mouse pushed in.

'You don't mind me shoving in, do you? I'm keen to get on with my practice.'

Bashar's queue barging hadn't gone unnoticed, and Ramesh brandished his serving spatula.

'Just you get to the back of the queue like everyone else, Bashar,' Ramesh reprimanded him. 'There's plenty to go around, and you'll just have to wait your turn.'

The young mouse did as he was told but prodded Bhoo, who was the smallest target, in the chest.

'Don't think I won't forget that, shrimp,' he said menacingly.

They were all shocked by his behaviour when everybody else had been so nice up till now.

'Here, eat up,' said Sunni, putting a small round bun in Bhoo's paws. 'Woolly will be getting started any moment, and you don't want to keep him waiting... believe me.'

At that moment, Woolly boomed to all those around him and to some who weren't. Some startled faces appeared from the residences above them to see what all the commotion was about.

'Achha, so whoever's here for today's trial, please assemble in the middle of the ground as quick as you can. '

All the prospective players, even Bashar, meekly complied and jogged out to the middle of the ground.

'Come on, come and join us,' Sunni invited his new friends, who having exchanged an anxious look between themselves meekly complied. Woolly strode out to join them carrying a clipboard, which he hugged to his chest, protecting its secret.

'Today's trial will take the form of a double wicket game,' he announced. 'You'll be paired up and will bat as a team for a limited number of overs. In the meantime, the rest of you will bowl and field. The team for the upcoming match against the Mumbai Cricketeers is almost complete. You know what an important fixture it is, and there is just one position in the batting line-up to confirm. I will be announcing the team at the end of the practice.'

The players murmured among themselves, each of them trying to appear as nonchalant as possible about their prospects of being selected.

'Sunni, you're okay to make up the numbers and field?' Woolly singled out his utility substitute and general gofer.

'Yes indeed, Woolly bhai, and I have some cricket playing friends all the way from London, UK who are keen to play.'

'London is it?' Woolly said, taking a step closer to examine them.

'From Lord's Cricket Ground actually,' Compo said slightly pompously, which he instantly regretted.

'I'm afraid this isn't Lord's,' he bent down and ran his paw over the smooth green baize surface. 'No, this isn't the most famous ground in the world, but as a great man once said, "I feel the force in this field."'

If Woolly was trying to be inspirational, then it was certainly working. The onlookers were mesmerised, stunned into silence until one of them spoke.

'Was it Gandhiji?' said a wide-eyed mouse, referring to Mahatma Gandhi, the unofficial father of the country as an independent nation.

'No, Luke Skywalker,' he said airily. 'Now, are we here to play crrr...icket or aren't we?'

'YAYYYY!' they all cheered.

'Right, I'm going to pair you all up. My word is final, and they'll be no moaning or bickering,' said Woolly as he took a small pencil from behind his ear and started scribbling on his clipboard.

'Bashar, I'd like you to be paired with Bhupathi, or Bhoo as he is known. Our most experienced player with our newest recruit.'

'Him?' Bashar blurted. 'I wouldn't be seen dead on the pitch with him.'

'It can be arranged,' Woolly said darkly. 'So that is settled, and we'll hear no more on the subject.'

Woolly ran through the rest of the pairings before setting a field. He was pleased to have Beaky, Compo and Bumble as extra fieldsmen, as most of the trialists were keener to bat and bowl.

Mr Googly had appeared on the edge of the boundary, and Woolly made his way over to chat to him. The players did their best to appear as cool as possible whilst they were actually really desperate to know what they were discussing.

With a handshake, Woolly broke away from his conversation and jogged out to the middle.

'First pair up—Chiku and Devall.'

He set about placing the rest of the players in the field as the opening pair strode out to the wicket. He tucked Bhoo just behind square on the leg side. Here he would get a good view of the game and have time to set himself to field if the ball came his way. He took no chances with his English volunteers, sending each of them to long leg, deep midwicket and third man. It was hardly a vote of confidence, but they were all pleased to be involved.

Lambu, a tall mouse with the shaggiest, most unruly mop of fur on the top of his head had been given the ball. He paced out a lengthy run and waited for Woolly to get the practice started. With the batsman having taken block and the field set, Woolly took his place as the umpire at the bowler's end and called 'Play!'

Lambu didn't need telling twice and tore up to the wicket. He released the ball with a whippy action, delivering it at pace. Having pitched, it sailed past the batsman without interfering with him. The ball had stopped rotating, and it appeared to fall through the air frozen as a snapshot. Mahi, the wicketkeeper, followed the ball intently. His eyes widened as it honed in on him, meeting his gloves with an intimidating smack.

'Too quick for you?' Woolly goaded the batsman.

But Devall wasn't listening. Seemingly unflappable, he simply settled over his bat, head bowed, waiting for the next ball. Lambu raced in again, this time erring slightly down the leg-side. Devall picked the ball off his pads effortlessly and his partner called for a run. Chiku, in contrast to his partner, was all confidence and swagger. He prowled around the crease almost taunting the fielding side to come at him. Sure enough, when the next ball was slightly over-pitched, he drove it back smartly between the bowler and the umpire.

So the pairings came and went. All the time Woolly noted their strengths and their foibles. As he watched, Mr Googly gave little away from his vantage point on the boundary. It was impossible to read anything from a nod of his head, a tip of his hat or an adjustment of his spectacles.

The next pair at the wicket comprised a burly looking fellow called Yoovi and a quirky looking character called Bhadbhat. The latter was on strike. Behind the stumps, Mahi raised his eyebrows as he settled to his mark without taking a guard. Bhadbhat had a sheepish look about him, and if asked, one would say that he looked out of place. The reason for that was exactly that. Woolly had broken his own steadfast rule, that the trials were attended only on merit. He'd caved in to the incessant badgering of his Auntyji to have a look at the youngster. Now here he was, about to face some of the best bowling Mumbai's mouse cricket scene had to offer. Sure enough, the outcome was predictable, swift and sadly not painless. Bhadbhat managed to fend a rising ball from Gopu, another fast bowler, up under his helmet and took a sharp blow to the snout. Luckily, Nani, the team physio, was on hand to attend to his injury. There was a little blood and fortunately no teeth were lost, and once he'd been helped off the ground, the practice started again.

Now, for many of those in attendance, came the main event. The interesting last pairing of the team's top batsman, Bashar and Bhoo, the young upstart from the wrong part of town.

'I'm wishing you all the very best of luck,' Bhoo stuttered nervously as they walked out to the middle. Bashar didn't respond. He simply held his bat up in the air and gave it twiddle before heading to the non-striker's end.

For Woolly, the practice had gone remarkably well. His young guns had performed admirably, confirming his own ability to spot talent. Of course, in the limited overs format that they played, he wasn't just looking at the manner in which they made their runs. The ability to accumulate and keep the scoreboard moving was essential. This put extra pressure on the players, but if this was the case, Bhoo wasn't showing it. Now in his element, he went through his pre-delivery ritual, taking guard, surveying the field and settling into his stance, all the time muttering his mantra... 'Watch the ball.'

On the boundary, Uncle was feeling enough tension for the two of them. He involuntarily mimed a defensive stroke as the bowler started his run up. He needn't have worried. Beneath his little helmet, for Bhoo, time slowed, and he almost had time to chuckle himself. There were days when he found this game remarkably easy, and today was one of them. So keen was his eye that he could see which side of the ball the bowler had shined and how this might affect the delivery. As the ball arrived, he stepped towards it and the middle of his bat connected firmly with the ball. Finding a gap, there was an easy single on offer and he called 'YES!' firmly to his partner.

'NO!' Bashar replied and stood his ground. It was such an obvious run that Bhoo had already set off and had to scurry back to the safety of the crease.

Regaining his composure, he looked to his partner for some apology, but Bashar had turned his back on him. As the junior player, Bhoo was powerless, better to just put it out of his mind and get on.

The bowler returned to his mark, turned, ran in and bowled. A short, slower ball that sat up, asking to be whacked. Bhoo rocked onto his back foot and smashed it to mid-wicket. Although it went straight to the fielder, such was the force of the ball that it burst through his paws. Never run on a miss-field they say, but here was an easy single. Bashar wasn't interested, calling a resolute 'NO!' once again.

So it continued for the next two balls, further frustrating Bhoo in his bid to make it into the team. Bhoo squatted down on his haunches and rested his head against the handle of his bat. If he was going to make an impact, then he was going to have to do something out of the ordinary. Having taken a moment to reflect, once again he took his place in front of the stumps. The bowler delivered the next ball, and as it left his hand, Bhoo crouched in his stance. Using the bat as a ramp he flicked the ball over his shoulder and the wicketkeeper's head to the boundary. What spectators there were let out a gasp, which most of the mice in fielding positions echoed.

The improvised shot brought about a change in the field, and several players were pushed out on to the leg-side boundary. A long stop was placed behind the wicketkeeper to stop the previous unorthodox shot from happening again.

The bowler charged in and bowled. With the leg side packed with fielders, he was dismayed to see the ball swatted over the cover boundary on the off side. The 'switch hit' Bhoo had played relied upon him being able to hit the ball having changed from a right hand to a left-handed grip. It was a truly remarkable strike for such a little fellow.

The over came to an end, and the fieldsman adjusted their positions and a new bowler took the ball. At this time, the batsmen would normally meet for a midwicket powwow, pleasantries exchanged and a gloved fist pump. Bashar did not leave his crease. He instead busied himself with a little bit of 'gardening', tapping down imaginary lumps in the wicket with his bat.

There was a change of bowling and a tall mouse called Jumbo came on to bowl some leg spin. Bashar, now facing, was watchful and played the ball as it turned across him into a gap square of the wicket. The pair took an easy single without so much as a murmur from Bhoo. Fearing the same treatment from Bashar as in the previous over, and that once again he'd be becalmed, Bhoo took control of his destiny. His approach to playing leg spin was to stay light on his feet, to make frequent adjustments and work the ball around, dabbing and deflecting. At least this was how he started playing it. A deft dab sent the ball down to the third man boundary. The fielder at backward point was moved down to third man to stop him playing the shot again. He countered this with a full-blooded cut through the area the fielder had just been moved from. The next ball gave him an opportunity to show his defence, smothering a 'wrong 'un', a disguised ball that spun sharply towards him. This he followed with a little dance down the wicket before lofting the ball back over the bowler's head. Finally, he retained the strike by dropping the ball just in front of him and haring off with a cry of 'YES!'

Bashar, startled by Bhoo's commanding performance, for a moment forgot his resolve and complied. Starting on his heels, he just made his ground as the wicket was broken.

The trial had been a great success for Bhoo and his supporters. The rest of the team had enjoyed a good run out and everyone was buzzing.

'Very impressive, young mouse,' Woolly complimented him. 'That bat has quite a middle.'

'Oh yes, sir, it is a Very, Very, Special bat from AJ, Shahenshah of cricket bat making.'

'If it's from AJ, then it is indeed,' he said with a knowing smile.

As the players left the field, several of them ran over to congratulate Bhoo. The English mice were particularly complimentary.

'That was brilliant!' cried Compo.

'Stunning, really inventive,' Beaky agreed.

'Who'd have though such a little fella would run them ragged like that,' Bumble added.

Uncle walked out onto the pitch with his arms outstretched and greeted Bhoo with a hug.

'Well played, well played,' he enthused.

Another group of three mice on the boundary were less animated. They'd appeared partway through the practice session. Two huge mice flanked a tiny one, who had an 'Elvis style' quiff and wore dark glasses. It was Mr Doolally, the manager of the Mumbai

Cricketeers. One of his henchmen motioned for Bashar to join them as he left the field, which he did somewhat self-consciously.

'There appears to be a new kid on the block,' said Mr Doolally.

'Yaar,' Bashar drawled pensively.

'At this rate, you'll no longer be the star of the team. As I have said many times, you should come and join the Cricketeers.' If Mr Doolally was trying to get under Bashar's skin, he was doing a good job.

'The little guy came off today, but I hear he failed before, and no doubt he'll fail again. Remember, it only takes one ball, and it's all over.'

'Yes indeed, but the same could be said for you.'

'But I'm the captain; my place is secure.'

'I wouldn't be so sure of that. No one is indispensable. Let's get wonder boy over here and have a little chat.' Mr Doolally took out a comb and dragged it through is quiff.

'I'm having nothing to do with him. If you want to speak to him, you can get him yourself,' Bashar spat defiantly.

One of the henchmen took a step towards him.

'My dear Bashar, you won't be in anyone's team if you were to... let's say... get injured.' There was a hint of menace in Mr Doolally's tone.

Grudgingly, Bashar mooched off and returned with Bhoo, whom he'd had to prise from a gaggle of admirers.

'Introduce us please, Bashar,' Mr Doolally grinned.

'This is Bhupathi, or the so called 2½-inch run machine,' Bashar sneered and slunk off.

'Ha Ha! Run machine! I like it! It suits you if today's display is anything to go by. And do you know who I am?'

'No, Saabji,' Bhoo replied timidly.

'I, if I may say so, am 'Mr Cricket' in Mumbai. What do you think about that?'

'I'm not sure really. Well done to you, sir?'

'Ha Ha!' Mr Doolally boomed again. 'Oh, ho ho, "well done" indeed.' He pulled out a paisley patterned handkerchief and dabbed at his eye as if wiping away a tear. 'Now tell me, have you agreed to play for Mouse XI yet?' He was suddenly serious.

'I'm rather hoping that they'll ask me.'

'So you haven't, and they haven't asked you. *Good!*'

'That was my second trial and...' Bhoo looked suddenly bashful, '...and it did go quite well.'

'What if I asked you to play for my team, the Mumbai Cricketeers?'

'It would be an honour to be asked, sir. But the Bombay Yacht Club Mouse XI up to now has been very kind and accommodating. Even giving me a second chance after my first trial went badly. So to suddenly play for another team, especially without asking them, would be disloyal, I feel.'

'Disloyal? PAH! First come, first served I say. Do you or do you not want a guaranteed spot in my starting line up?' His tone was more aggressive than Bhoo was used to.

'As I say, sir, it is very flattering and nice to be asked. However, I have to say thank you, but no. Now if you please, I need to go to my Uncle.'

Bhoo made to join the others. They were milling around the playing area helping to clear the equipment and bits and pieces involved in the cricket game. As some of the players settled on the outfield, a collection of ladies, dressed in brightly coloured saris, appeared from the alcoves around the pitch.

Someone arrived with a bag full of Bhunna Channa, roasted chickpeas, 'borrowed' from a street vendor.

'Is this the cricket tea?' asked Bumble as he joined a group sharing out the roasted seeds. But no sooner had his bottom touched the ground than the gaggle of girls started to pester them.

'Don't get comfortable now, boys,' said Ayesha. 'Remember, we have the pitch now to practice our dance moves.'

'You guys have had your fun. You should be up there looking after the children. We can't rely on the grandparents,' Babi added, pointing to the alcoves that rose above them.

The boys got to their feet and started to mooch off towards the residences.

'Hold on a moment, we'll need some of them to help us out,' pointed out Tina. 'You'll join us, Bunni?' she suggested, accosting one of the players leaving the ground.

Bunni held up a paw to decline the invitation. Up until now, Bunni had kept a low profile. Playing in dark glasses positioned under the brim of a cap and very much keeping out of the limelight. Bunni understood that as far as getting into the starting line up went, there was little chance. If, however, anyone were to drop out, there might be an opportunity.

'Chiku then? You have the matinee idol looks,' Tina said, trying to sweet-talk him.

'Not me,' he said, hurrying away.

'I've suddenly become very busy,' said another player, backing away.

'In that case, we'll have to have...' she cast her eye about and spotted Beaky and Compo, who were now at a bit of a loss as to what to do. 'Here are a couple of fine fellows. Just what we need!'

'I've got one too,' cried another girl, Priya, who'd caught hold of Bumble.

'Yurp...!' He spluttered as he was almost whisked off his feet, having been forcibly grabbed by the scruff of the neck. 'Hey, what's goin' on?'

'You boys are going to learn to BOLLYWOOD DANCE!' the girls cried in unison.

'I don't think I'm up to that,' Beaky whined feebly.

'Sure you are; it's simple,' Ayesha enthused. 'Come on, Tina, Leena, Chanda, Tvisha, Priti, Mina, Priya, Rinky and Babi, let's show these guys.'

An elderly transistor radio was pressed into action, and as 'filmi' music drifted across the ground, the girls took their places. The dance troupe lined up in formation and proceeded to perform an energetic and elaborate routine. When they'd finished, Ayesha stepped forward to collect the boys.

'What we need you guys to do...' she puffed, slightly out of breath, 'is to...'

'Err... thanks but, no thanks,' Beaky broke in.

'If you think I'm going in for all that swirling about and head wobbling, you've got another thing coming,' Bumble insisted.

'Don't be daft, you two. It looks fun!' Compo fancied himself as a bit of a dancer and was keen to give it a go.

'It's really very simple; there are just a few moves you need to know to get started,' Ayesha explained as she lined the three mice up. 'Just follow my simple instructions, and off weee-yerr go!'

With accompanying actions, Ayesha chanted, 'Take and give, take and give, screw in the light bulb, and pat the dog, screw in the light bulb and pat the dog. Scratch like a cat, scratch like a cat and give to God.' She reached up with both hands. 'Give to the dog,' she reached down, 'give to God and give to the dog. Hand on hip and shake and swap. Coins are falling from the sky, coins are falling from the sky, from the sky. Pray and open and pray and open and shimmy and stop.'

Chaos ensued. Bumble patted Beaky like a dog, Beaky forgot to screw in the light bulb, and Compo stuck his finger in his own eye as imaginary coins rained down on them. 'The Bollywood Mousettes', as they liked to be called, thought it was hilarious. Ayesha was laughing so hard that she was barely able to choke out the compliment. 'Not bad for a first effort.' Before she collapsed with laughter again.

However, the fun was quickly brought to an end by Uncle, who shuffled up as fast as he was able and gasped, 'Bhoo has been taken...'

Woolly

## Chapter Nine

The August of 1915 had been unseasonably cool and wet. The men of the 125th Napier Rifles were making their way back behind the line. They'd been relieved and had wound their way back to safety through numerous lines of communications trenches. Weighed down with equipment, the going had been slow, picking their way through their comrades and the debris of war.

On their way through the meandering trench system, one of the men had tripped and fallen heavily. Bilal Singh was what one might describe as a big unit. It was assumed that as a great big fellow, he was somehow immune to the hardships the men suffered. In fact, the deprivations of the front had a more profound effect on him physically. Struggling to regain his feet, a fellow soldier had helped him up. Sanjeev Kumar was an altogether different specimen, slight, lean, wiry and weather-beaten. He was the least likely soldier to come to Bilal's aid, and yet he'd been the quickest person to react.

Eventually, they were in the open, and they marched in a column with a steady sway. The sun burnt though the cloud and warmed the weary soldiers. Sanjeev found himself next to the man he'd helped.

'Can you smell that?' Sanjeev asked of the big man.

'No?' Bilal Singh replied, wondering what the spindly looking creature beside him was on about.

'Precisely, magnificent, isn't it?' Sanjeev declared as he inhaled deeply and let out his breath with a satisfied 'Aaahh.'

The smell of the trenches was indescribable, created by the coming together of many things, not least the men themselves. Eventually, they became immune to it. Now away from the front, the sour smell of their bodies made them wrinkle their noses.

'Do you hear that?' Bilal countered.

Sanjeev cocked his head to one side. 'Birds?'

'Yes, birds. There aren't many on the front line. You may have noticed.' Bilal looked down at his companion with a crooked smile.

As they marched, they talked of home. Of people and comforts they missed and their shared love of cricket. Later, when they reached the encampment, they surrendered their uniforms. Wrapped in coarse blankets, they waited their turn for baths in huge vats of hot water.

Their uniforms were put through delousing machines, steam treated to kill the parasites that plagued the men. As the last surviving 'Tommy' described them, 'The lice were the size of grains of rice, each with its own bite, each with its own itch.' For the time being, the men got relief from their irritation and were given suits of a sterilised blue material.

Bathed and clothed, the men flopped down on the grass with soldiers from other companies.

'Come on, you lot, look lively,' ordered a gruff sergeant major instructor carrying a sack over one shoulder. 'Which one of you 'orrible little men isn't going to get involved in my game.' He emptied the contents of a sack onto the grass and cast an eagle eye around the group. Stumps, a bat and a ball spilled out. 'Sport,' he continued, 'good for mind, body and soul.'

The men were used to a spot of football. It was an easy game to play spontaneously. One only needed a ball and a couple of tunics for goalposts. Cricket, however, would take a little more organising.

'Collins and Jonesie were professional cricketers before the war, Sarge,' one of the men piped up.

'And if you please, sir, many of the Indian jawans (young soldiers) love to play cricket,' Sanjeev ventured.

'Well ain't that luverly; we can have our own international test match on this nice stretch of grass here,' the sergeant major grinned.

The men all cheered, and two teams were picked from those lying around. The two former professional cricketers organised the England XI, and a hulking great sardar called Yogesh Singh took charge of the Indian side. Eventually, despite the claims of some of the men to be 'world-class' and the protests of others who didn't want to play, two teams were assembled.

The sergeant major flipped a coin, Yogesh called 'heads' correctly and the Indian side elected to bat.

'So what are we playing for, Sarge?' asked the wicketkeeper as the sergeant major took up his place as umpire.

The grizzled veteran thought for a moment. 'I've just the thing, a nice pile of new 'grey back' shirts for the winning team.'

The delousing of the uniforms rarely worked. Eggs, remaining in the fabric, would hatch within hours of the clothes being put on again. So to have a brand-new shirt would be a prize indeed.

'I have this,' called Bilal, holding up a small wooden elephant.

The sergeant major took it off him and examined it.

'This 'ere h'elephant has travelled all the way from Ind'juh, has it?'

'From Bombay, sir.'

'So we should call it the Bombay Trophy,' the sergeant major observed wisely.

The boundaries were determined as a line of trees on one side of the wicket and a stream on the other. With that, the game began. Jonesie, who in peacetime had opened the bowling for Kent, dismissed one of the Indian opening batsman with the first ball of the game.

'Out for a golden! That there trophy should be called the Bombay-Duck,' chirped the wicketkeeper, which got a laugh from players and spectators alike.

The game continued in good spirits, but it was soon clear that luck more than skill would determine the outcome. All over the field were little seedlings that acted like extra fielders. A good shot might go unrewarded. Likewise, a miss-hit might score a run just because the fielder was felled by an unseen rabbit hole or sapling.

Bowlers resorted to full tosses to negate the uneven bounce of the wicket. This favoured the more burly players, who clubbed the ball to the boundary. Catches were dropped, ends of fingers numbed and muscles pulled. Above all, everyone forgot, for a short time at least, why they were there and what was going on around them.

The Indian XI had posted a modest total of 80 for the loss of all 10 wickets, many of them run out. In reply, the England team had sportingly opened with two spindly looking characters. The first of these missed his first ball and then swung himself off his feet, knocking over his stumps trying to hit the second. The other opener fared no better, stopping a beamer with his forehead, which required immediate medical treatment. One of the ex-professionals took control and knocked the ball about in a confident manner. However, as he nudged the score along, dark clouds gathered, and eventually the match had to be abandoned due to the subsequent thunderstorm.

The players ran from the pitch laughing and sheltered under whatever they could find. Soon enough, they'd be packing their kit and marching back up the line. The trophy was never presented, and perhaps the sergeant major had clean shirts for a fortnight. So it was that a knock-about game slipped into the annals of time. Forgotten as well as remembered. Memories of it embellished and distorted into something far more momentous and celebrated.

The folklore surrounding the 'trenches' cricket match may have been warranted, or the story may have become combined with that of another match later that year—an altogether grander affair between and English XI and an Indian team watched by 40,000 people. This game, however, didn't take place on an area of open land spotted with self-sown plants in France. It took place 4,000 miles away at the Bombay Gymkhana.

A hundred years later on that same ground, the England team was hard at work practicing for its upcoming series of games. Gogi Singh had decided to take some time out of his day to wander up past the Law Courts to watch them. However, the sun was high in the sky, and already he felt his shirt start to stick to him. The sound of an auto rickshaw or tuk tuk over his shoulder suggested to him that it was worth the few bucks to be driven just up the road. He turned round to hail it and was amazed to find a pristine tuk tuk painted white with black dots like a Dalmatian. It was the most splendid tuk tuk he'd ever seen. Driven by a chauffeur complete with cap, its sole cargo was a wicker cage on the back seat. This contained what appeared to be, to use the collective noun, a mischief of mice. Surely the driver could squeeze him in, thought Gogi, but the man studiously ignored all attempts to attract his attention.

Gogi gave up, deciding that the walk would do him good and that there was plenty to see on the way. What was playing at the Regal Cinema, what the kerb side hawkers had on offer and if any bits had crumbled off the Gothic façade of the High

Court Building. You could usually bank on finding some sort of unusual goings on if just watching the world go by in Mumbai. Sure enough, he came across two pairs of workmen armed with ladders attempting to string a banner across the street.

'Take care up that ladder,' he advised one of them cheerily.

'I'll be fine, so long as my friend holds it nice and steady,' the man replied with a smile.

The banner drooped for the time being across the road and various vehicles ran over it, leaving tyre imprints. The words 'Jaldi Chalo' were emblazoned across it.

'What is it for?' Gogi asked.

'The cricket game at the weekend, tying to generate interest in the Commemorative Match to raise money, I guess,' the workman shrugged.

Gogi wanted to say that he knew all about it. That he was going to be a guest of honour, but he had second thoughts. He didn't want to be seen to be boasting. Instead, he watched for a while as the two groups hoisted the banner into position.

'JALDI CHALO—LET'S FIND THIS GAME A PRIZE
MRS CHATTERJEE'S CHAPATI FLOUR PLEASED TO SUPPORT
THE BOMBAY BROTHERS' CENTENARY CRICKET MATCH'

Holes had been cut in the banner to stop it acting as a sail, but the message was clear enough. Although a giant silver chapatti as a prize for the winning team seemed an unlikely solution to the objective set by the DJ on the radio. Gogi saluted the men as they tied the banner into position and carried on his way. In no time, he arrived at Azad Maidan. Stretching out in front of him were 25 acres of dusty sports ground known for its cricket pitches. At its southern end were the gymkhana grounds and the long Bombay Gymkhana Clubhouse, built in 1875.

A reasonable crowd had gathered along the fence separating the carefully manicured grounds of the old club from the public space. Here nets had been erected, and the England players were being put through their paces. Their garish modern training kit was at odds with the old style of the mock Tudor building behind them.

Not far away, Moti Kumar had being attending an assistant stationmaster's annual railway operations training and assessment course. The venue for this was the Chhatrapati Shivaji Terminus, or CST. Formerly known as Victoria Terminus or VT, the gothic Victorian landmark is the hub of the city's train network. Behind the grand façade of the building, he'd spent a long hot morning in a stifling room. Just one rickety ceiling fan had beaten at the hot torpid air.

It was with some relief that he walked from the cathedral-like entrance of the station. He snaked his way through the gaggle of people making their way in and out of the station. It was a happy coincidence that the England cricket team were practicing nearby, and he was keen to get a glimpse of the players in action. It was a short walk to Azad Maidan, although the busy road was not the easiest to cross. The assortment of vehicles was varied, and although there were safer places to cross, Moti backed himself to take the most direct route. Every Mumbaiker has a pretty good repertoire of moves to avoid traffic. A sidestep, dodge or shimmy, so Moti was shocked, having picked a gap in the traffic, to be swamped by a wave of the city's black and yellow cabs. A traffic light up the road had released them, and they suddenly swarmed about him. He swayed and feinted like a boxer to find his way round them, only to encounter a double decker bus rumbling up the inside lane. He was too quick for it and sprinted past the front of it only to find a white tuk tuk whirring up behind it. There was no way to miss it, and the driver took no evasive action. The contact was sharp but glancing, and although shocked by it, Moti made it to the side of the road. The tuk tuk carried on its way, and he watched the unusually painted auto rickshaw disappear into the traffic.

'That, old man, was too close for comfort,' he admonished himself and limped off towards the playing fields. He passed under a banner advertising the upcoming game at the weekend.

'GLEAMO TOOTHPASTE – SUPPORTS THE BOMBAY
BROTHERS' CRICKET
JALDI CHALO - # WINNERS'

He wasn't sure what '#WINNERS' meant—social media wasn't his thing—but he remembered the radio broadcast. Obviously, the DJ's idea to whip up local support and get behind the Centenary Game was getting some traction.

The bash to his leg he'd received from the tuk tuk was painful, but he felt sure he could walk it off. A path cut diagonally through the straw-coloured, sun-dried grass of Azad Maidan, where a number of cricket matches were underway, and as he made his way across it, he encountered a tiny little boy tottering along.

'He's walking across India,' his father, an English tourist armed with a camera, called out from a few paces away. What had seemed out of place made sense. Moti gave the boy a friendly pat on the head.

'He's making a good job of it. I'm just on my way to see his countrymen at their cricket practice.'

He pointed to a sizeable crowd that had gathered along a fence dividing the public space from the grounds of the Bombay Gymkhana Club.

'We may join you if I can get him to change direction,' the intrepid toddler's Dad joked.

Moti made his way to the fence and tried to find a decent vantage point. Those who'd arrived earlier were not keen to give up the space they'd secured. He edged his way into the melee and bobbed up and down, straining to get a view. Eventually, he squeezed into a space and got a glimpse of the three nets that had been pegged out for the players to practice in. He was mentally ticking off in his mind the players he recognised when someone tapped him on the shoulder.

'Excuse me, but you're bleeding,' a man said in a matter-of-fact way.

Moti looked down, and sure enough, blood had seeped through his trousers.

'Oh my goodness, I've just been clipped by a crazy tuk tuk driver. I could have sworn he actually tried to hit me.'

'Whatever he was trying to do, he certainly succeeded

in taking a chunk out of you,' Gogi Singh said, taking a neatly pressed handkerchief from his pocket. 'Here, let me help you.'

So a hundred years on, the two Bombay Brothers' descendants unwittingly exchanged roles, one helping the other.

Two miles away, the spotted tuk tuk arrived at its destination of Chor Bazaar, the flea market. It turned into the end of Mutton Street, and the driver stopped the engine. There was no point in trying to get a vehicle down the crowded narrow street. A cow sat obstinately blocking one side of the entrance, and two oil-smeared youths were dismantling a scooter on the other. Chor Bazaar, a glorious muddle of dusty shops crammed with bric-a-brac, antiques of dubious antiquity, car parts and junk. Here, a mass of passers-by mingled with local shopkeepers of the loveable rogue variety, stray pi-dogs and the odd goat. The driver, Bhuman, adjusted his mirrored, aviator style sunglasses and set off down the street. In his hand the wicker cage draped with a red velvet cover. Halfway down, he stopped outside number 26, a building with a shuttered entrance beneath a crumbling frontage bearing the wording *'Cricket Curios'*. A rusty key opened a smaller shabby door to one side of the shutter, its peeling paint showing the many colours it had been through time. The door unlocked, Bhuman briefly looked both up and down the street before disappearing inside.

Inside the *'Cricket Curios'* emporium, shadowy shelves stood sentry. Bhuman flicked a switch and a single light bulb illuminated the area. The shelves were stacked with dented trophies and odd bits and pieces of sad-looking cricket odds and ends. These items were not for sale, merely a smokescreen for the main business activity.

Behind the shelves at the back of the shop, a heavy curtain obscured an unlikely secret. With the flick of a second light switch, a florescent tube light stuttered and burst into life, revealing a vintage Rolls Royce.

Beaky

## Chapter Ten

It had taken a while for them to calm Uncle down. Woolly found him something to sit on, and Nani produced her wet sponge, with its restorative magic, from her physio's bag. Eventually, he was able to recount what had happened.

'At the end of the practice, Bhoo was talking to a little fellow who was accompanied by two suspicious-looking characters. I'd seen them during the game and thought that they had the look of ne'er-do-wells.'

There was a short exchange amongst the assembled mice, who needed to establish just what a 'ne'er-do-well' was, settling on 'bad guy', which explained just about everything.

'While everyone was getting ready for tea and you young ladies were coming out, I'd walked out to the wicket to wait for Bhoo. The pushy boy whom he batted with had taken him over there. But after he'd left them, there seemed to be a bit of a commotion, and the next thing I know, they've picked up Bhoo and carted him off.'

'Bashar...?' Woolly called out. 'Can you shed any light on what's going on?'

But Bashar was nowhere to be found. He'd slunk away, having guessed that Mr Doolally had decided to make a new acquisition for his team.

'What did they look like?' asked Ayesha.

'The little one looked like a small Elvis Presley,' Uncle described Mr Doolally to a T.

'Yes, I saw them arrive towards the end of the practice,' Sunni added. 'I thought they'd just turned up to snoop on us before the big game.'

'If you know who took him, can't we just go and get him back?' Compo suggested.

'You might think that would be the answer,' Woolly said, waving to Mr Googly.

Mr Googly strolled over.

'Why all the long faces? I thought the practice went particularly well,' Mr Googly beamed.

'It seems Mr Doolally has kidnapped our 2½-inch run machine,' Woolly explained.

'Ah,' Mr Googly replied knowingly.

'The youngsters want to know why, if Mr Doolally has decided to abduct their teammate, that we just don't go and get him back. Perhaps you can enlighten them as to why that isn't such a simple course of action.'

Mr Googly explained that, surprisingly for a mouse, Mr Doolally was an individual of means. He had, despite the fact that their world had no call for it, amassed a considerable fortune. In short, he had cash, enabling him to enjoy some of the trappings of the human world.

'This is no ordinary mouse we are dealing with. This is the 'Mr Big' of Mumbai's mouse world. Complete with human sidekicks, transport and a secret hideout.'

'You are pulling my leg!' an astonished Bumble spluttered. 'Let's get after him, right now!'

'I fear there is nothing we can do but wait,' Mr Googly said seriously. 'If Doolally wants to play him in the game, we can negotiate his return then. If he just wants to keep him out of the game, then we have another problem on our hands.'

At this, Ayesha and Babi gasped and Tina burst into tears.

'Getting in a flap isn't going to help anyone,' Woolly reasoned. 'We've all got an exciting evening ahead, so I suggest everyone calm down. We put the cricket stuff away, the girls sort themselves out, and the rest of you make yourselves useful looking after the children.'

'What's going on this evening?' Compo asked.

'There is a big reception for the England team in their hotel. Many of us are planning to go over to see the players,' Sunni explained.

'Also there's going to be all sorts of Bollywood royalty in attendance,' Babi said dreamily.

'Music, dancing, A-list celebrities and the hotel's finest nibbles,' Ayesha purred.

'How can you be thinking of dancing and high jinx when my Bhupathi has been abducted?' Uncle demanded with a look of consternation.

'You're quite right,' Woolly observed. 'However, everyone has been looking forward to this evening for some time, and I think, therefore, that those who want to should be allowed to go. In the meantime, Uncle, let's sit down and formulate some course of action. Whether it is, just to sit tight and wait...'

'Just sit and wait!' Uncle exploded, interrupting him, in response to which Woolly held up a calming hand like a traffic policeman.

'Or... we plan to take more definite action.'

'Might we join your meeting?' Compo ventured. 'We've had a not dissimilar situation at home in London when a friend of ours went missing. We too found ourselves being bullied by the local heavies.'

Compo remembered the time Willow, the Lord's mouse colony's bat maker, had gone missing. Then she was used as a bargaining chip, but that had worked in their favour, buying them time and bringing about a momentous win at their 'win-at-all-costs' cricket match. This had ultimately put them in a position to play to their strengths, although outmuscled, they'd won out in the end.

'You're more than welcome,' Woolly replied.

So it was decided and everyone went their separate ways.

Later that evening, mice from all over the colony descended on the cricket pitch. The meeting had proved inconclusive, and its attendees sat disconsolately on the outfield. Soon they disappeared into a milling throng of excited little fur balls, all of whom had assembled to make their way through the long pipe to the hotel.

'I hate that pipe,' Mina said disdainfully. 'Here we are, all dressed up and we have to make our way up that mucky old pipe.'

The girl's had made the most of their night out amongst Mumbai's glitterati and were looking lovely in their colourful saris.

'I'd ferry you in my rickshaw,' Sunni offered, 'but there are just too many of us.'

'We'll be fine,' Ayesha sensibly intervened.

They set off in a long line, members of the cricket team, the girls' dance troupe, Compo, Beaky and Bumble, and a host of assorted cricket and Bollywood film fans from the colony with Woolly bringing up the rear.

They'd made the journey before and were well practised at scurrying up the pipe with only the dot of light ahead to guide them. Once in the hotel, their progress through the old building was relatively simple through the ducts of the air-conditioning system.

In the foyer, preparations had been made all day for the big evening. A stage had been built, overhung with a banner greeting the England cricket team. Seating fanned out from it to accommodate the great and the good who would be attending. To one side, a small interview area had been set aside, decked out with a garish backdrop and surrounded by TV lights.

A steady flow of vehicles deposited its occupants at the hotel's entrance. The whole foyer had been decked out as befitted such a glittering occasion. Strings of lights, garlands and arrangements of flowers were in abundance. Several photographers hovered around and a small group, 'Tinie Tabla', played a synth-pop-Asian-elevator-fusion backing track to the whole scene.

In the foyer, the murmur of the guests chatter increased to a roar. Behind a screen separating him from the rest of the foyer stood Duke Patel undergoing a series of deep breathing exercises. Star of the recent hit film *'Breakfast in Maximum City',* he was more comfortable in front of the camera than in public. Giving his head a final shake and blowing out like a horse, he picked up the radio microphone and stepped out from behind the screen.

'GOOD EVEE-VER-NING, PEOPLE,' he boomed. 'Have we got a treat for you?'

The gathered guests responded with a pleasing 'WHOOOO!'

'It is my pleasure to introduce *Mumbai Thumka.*' A brightly dressed dance troupe mounted the stage.

By now, the mice had arrived in the foyer. They'd passed through an air-conditioning vent and had lined up along a decorative valance below the ceiling.

The girls clapped in delight at the sight of the *Mumbai Thumka* dancers. They were performing a well-known number from a popular film, and soon the Bollywood Mousettes were copying them with their own version high above the audience.

As the dance came to an end, Duke stepped forward once again and breathed into the microphone.

'Now for the reason we're all here. Put your hands together and welcome the England cricket team!'

The players entered the space and lined up at the base of the stage, where they stood somewhat awkwardly. The crowd's welcome was polite without being over the top—they were the opposition after all. But for a cricket-loving public, International cricketers, wherever they hail from, will always be a curiosity.

Certainly that was the case amongst the mousey cricketers present, and for one in particular, the reminder of home was too much.

'I have to get closer,' blurted Beaky. It was out of character, as he was usually so cautious, but there was no stopping him.

'No wait!' Compo called, but it was too late.

Meanwhile, Duke Patel was in full flow.

'Perhaps the England captain would like to join me in front of the cameras? We're very excited to be broadcasting live to several countries tonight, and viewers have been texting their questions.'

As the England captain stepped tentatively into the limelight, Beaky shot off along the valance. There was nothing else for it, and so Compo gave chase, and in a 'if you can't beat 'em join 'em' sort of way, Bumble set off too.

A common mouse can run as fast as 7.5 to 8 mph. Such speeds would be equivalent to a 5-foot 10-inch human being running more than 160 mph. As a result, the short distance between their vantage point and Beaky's intended destination was covered in no time. Compo and Bumble arrived just in time to watch him make the leap from the valance to the top of the backdrop framed by the TV camera. Compo and Bumble exchanged a quick glance that was full of meaning and made the same leap.

Below them, Duke's interview was underway.

'You've been to Mumbai before, haanji?'

'Yes indeed, many times. I'm a great fan of the food,' replied the captain diplomatically.

'Mumbai is quite a city. How is it different to say, London?'

'Certainly in terms of the animals one encounters during the day, there is quite a difference. For example, today I've seen an elephant, a goat, several dogs, a cow holding up the traffic and three mice.'

'Acha, that is India for you, sir. But three mice… that is very exact. Where did you see them?'

The England captain drew a point to a spot just above Duke's head.

'Just there...'

Duke looked above and behind him. There on the top of the backdrop were indeed three neat little mice, and if he wasn't mistaken, they were all wearing hats.

'What the...?" For a moment, Duke was lost for words. Eventually, his scrambled senses sorted themselves out and he shouted, 'SECURITY!'

Instant pandemonium ensued, and several guards arrived from several directions. The England captain showed impeccable footwork and stepped to one side. Duke flailed about as if swatting a fly. At the same time, the cameraman attempted to stop the backdrop collapsing with one arm whilst continuing to film from his shoulder-held camera. In fact, he succeeded at neither, getting some fantastic footage of the underside of Duke Patel's nose while the backdrop collapsed on him. Beaky, Compo and Bumble had escaped injury by reacting as soon as first spotted. They'd managed to leap clear to the safety of the valance before scurrying back to their friends.

Back in England, all was quiet on St John's Wood Road. In the night-watchman's cabin behind the high wall surrounding Lord's Cricket ground, Gary Nicholls was tuning his TV to

*World Cricket Roundup.* As ever, he had several uninvited guests lurking in the shadows as Victor Agnew, the show's compere, made his report.

'This evening, a reception held to welcome the England team to Mumbai, India was disrupted by the appearance of three uninvited guests. If you just watch the following film and look above the man with the microphone, you'll see what I mean.'

The footage played out and captured on camera for the entire world to see were Beaky, Compo and Bumble. In the darkness, the eyes of the small visitors widened and their jaws dropped open.

The programme cut back to the presenter. 'Ho, ho, ho, looks like it all got pretty chaotic after that. Hopefully the upcoming series will be as eventful but with less broken furniture involved... and now to our next item...'

Lit by the blue blinking glow of the TV set up on a bookshelf, Beefy broke the stunned silence amongst the mice.

'India, he definitely said India, didn't he?' His gruff voice was not best suited to a whisper.

'How on earth did they get there?' WG asked bewilderedly.

'More to the point, how are we going to get them back?' asked Don bleakly.

## Chapter Eleven

Despite the unexpected sideshow, which unfortunately was broadcast across the globe, the reception at the hotel had been a success. The local newspapers would the next day run a headline 'Jaldi Chalo' or 'Let's get ready to rumble' and a photo of Duke Patel looking dishevelled. The footage would also become a quick fire hit on *YouTube*. But for the most part, the invitees had left the event fed, watered and happy to have met and had access to the England cricket stars. The procession of vehicles that had deposited them materialised one by one and whisked their passengers off into the Mumbai night.

The mice had made their way back home too. A headcount to make sure that everyone was present and correct had revealed that Sunni wasn't amongst them. He'd got chatting to another group of mice who'd had the same idea about gate-crashing the event and then missed the long convoy home. In due course, he'd appeared only to find that his absence had created a bit of a fuss.

'Where have you been?' barked Woolly. 'We were all worried.'

'Yes, we've lost quite enough little mice for one day,' Ayesha observed, which made Uncle wince.

'I'm really sorry, but I got talking about this and that to a little guy called Jeet at the cricket team reception. He lives in Mr Filippo's shop behind the hotel.'

Filippo, the shirt maker's shop was a slightly ramshackle establishment in Tulloch Road behind the hotel. It was just off the bustling Colaba Causeway with its numerous small shops and footpath outlets that sold everything under the sun. Here, life was far more raw and tough due to the large numbers of ravenous stray dogs and cats. To survive in this environment for long, a house mouse had to be very canny indeed.

'Jeet knows all sorts of things about what goes on in the area which happily pass us by. He was saying that Mr Doolally has a reputation as the 'Big Cheese' of Mumbai Mousedom.'

'We all know that,' Woolly snorted. 'He seems to be able to do pretty much exactly what he wants at any given time.' Uncle nodded in agreement.

'Yes but, when I say Cheese—I mean *cheese*. He is the biggest seller of illegally sourced cheese in the city,' Sunni explained.

'Mice have a reputation in the world for liking cheese, but it isn't something we have much access to,' Ayesha chipped in.

'Precisely, because there isn't any spare lying around.

Doolally has an army of mice collecting it from hotels, restaurants, clubs and even as far out as the airport.'

'But what does he do with all this cheese?' Woolly asked.

'He sells it, don't you see?' Sunni sounded exasperated.

'Yes, but what for?' Woolly and Ayesha chorused.

'Money, people money, banknotes, coins... whatever his furry clients can get their paws on. Anything will do. It's easier to get hold of than cheese, and because they can't tell what a note is worth, he does rather well. He might get a five rupee note or a thousand rupee note and everything in between.'

'So that explains how he has his own tuk tuk and driver. It did always seem pretty extraordinary,' Woolly murmured, twiddling his whiskers in a distracted manner as if they were a twirly moustache.

'If this Jeet fellow knows so much about Mr Doolally, does he know where he lives? Perhaps he can lead us to Bhoo,' Uncle suggested.

'He does indeed. Mr Doolally's cheese operation is run from the back of a shop called *Cricket Curios* in Chor Bazaar.'

'Righto, let's go!' declared Uncle, marching off.

'Hold it right there,' Woolly ordered, catching the old mouse by his tail. 'Chor Bazaar is a long way from here, and if we're going to save Bhoo, just charging off into the night isn't going to help anyone. Let's all sleep on it and regroup in the morning.'

Grudgingly Uncle stood down and the little party split up, making their way to their separate quarters.

The time difference between Mumbai and London, 4,466 miles away, is four and a half hours. As a result, dawn was breaking in Mumbai as the late-night TV watchers in London got to grips with the idea that their friends were alive. Of course, they were eager to pass on the good news and they'd scooted out of the night-watchman's cabin and sprinted home. To save time, they'd taken the more direct but more risky route across the ground's hallowed turf. Finally, they went up through the pipe from the Lord's playing surface known as the 'thunderbox', disappearing into the fabric of the old pavilion. They'd squirmed through the entrance hole of the mouse residence, bursting into the well-worn mousey corridor that served the secret world and maze of rooms.

'EVERYONE! EVERYONE! FANTASTIC NEWS!' Beefy shouted.

A host of little heads peeked out from the dormitories. Don and WG echoed the call.

'Our friends are alive and well!' cried Don.

'Who, what, where?' spluttered CMJ vaguely.

'Compo, Beaky and Bumble, they're in India!' WG added.

'In where?' spluttered Ranji in disbelief.

Don recounted how they'd just watched them on the nightwatchman's TV.

'But how do you know it was really India?' Ranji asked.

'Because the England captain was in the same picture, and we all know where the England team is right now,' Don exclaimed excitedly.

As avid supporters of the team, a number of them chorused, 'In India.'

As the excited mice discussed the news, Willow edged her way over to Don.

'Is it really true, Don?' she asked with tears in her eyes.

'Yes, really!' He put his paw on her shoulder to raise her spirits.'

'At least they're alive and well. But we'll never see them again, will we?' she said sadly.

This was true, but Don didn't have the heart to confirm her worst fears.

'They got themselves there... maybe they can get themselves back.'

But he could see from the droop in her shoulders as she wandered away from him that she wasn't convinced.

So on both sides of the world, the news was bittersweet. Each little colony was presented with hope balanced against impossible odds.

For the meantime, in Mumbai at least, the worry of those odds was eased by the prospect of breakfast.

As the mice emerged from their slumbers, they found that Woolly had attached a notice to the cricket ground's scoreboard. It read:

Bombay Yacht Club (Mouse XI)

v

Mumbai Cricketeers Invitational XI

PROVISIONAL

| Bunni | Chiku |
| Dervall | Mahi |
| Yoovi | Gabbar |
| Bhupathi | Bhajji |
| Lambu | Jumbo |
| Ishy | Sunni (twelfth man) |

The list created quite a stir. Everyone who went up and read it gave the same reaction, a visible twitch and sharp intake of breath. It was unthinkable, but Woolly had done it. He'd dropped Bashar. It was a controversial selection, but Woolly had picked the team on talent, attitude and application.

When Bashar finally appeared, there was a shiver of anticipation amongst the onlookers as to how he'd react. Woolly had been looking out for him and strode out to the scoreboard to defend his decision.

Bashar rounded on him as he approached.

'PROVISIONAL! I'll say it's provisional! You don't even know if one of the players is still alive!'

'Well, if that is your attitude, then it looks as though I've made a good call. You're a good player, Bashar, but you're not indispensable. A little bit of humility goes a long way, so perhaps you should think about showing some.'

'I'm going to speak to Mr Googly about this.'

'Mr Googly is in complete agreement. No one player is bigger than the team.'

At that moment, Mr Doolally and a couple of his goons appeared at the other side of the ground.

'Cooee...!' he called. 'You don't mind us letting ourselves in.'

But Woolly did mind.

'You've a nerve showing your face here!' Woolly barked.

Mr Doolally looked perplexed.

'Where is our little run machine? What have you done with Bhupathi?'

'Who-pathi?' Doolally replied airily. If he was hiding Bhoo, he was certainly playing things pretty cool.

'Don't you play the innocent with me, Doolally, I've known you too long.' Woolly's tone was sufficiently threatening for the two goons to step forward as a barrier between the two mice. But before any nastiness ensued, Bashar, who'd sidled over, butted in.

'Might I have a word, Mr Doolally?'

'Of course, Bashar. I believe Woolly and I have finished our little chat.'

While Bashar and Mr Doolally talked, the three English visitors came to Woolly's aid.

'Are you all right, old son? It looks like things were getting pretty heated just then,' Bumble asked.

'That rotter Doolally, smarming his way in here. I can't believe he has the nerve. He must have Bhoo, and yet he's happy to swan in here as if nothing has happened.' Woolly kicked at the ground in disgust.

'Of course he has the youngster. On top of that, he's trying to get you riled and the team unsettled. By the looks of things, he's succeeding,' said Compo.

'You're right,' Woolly agreed. 'We need to stay on his good side.'

Mr Doolally approached them again, this time with Bashar, whom he had his arm around.

'So, Bashar here tells me that you no longer require his services, and as a result, he has accepted an offer to play for my side.'

'If that's what he wants, we'll be sorry to see him go, but so be it.' Woolly bit his lip, trying to conceal his displeasure.

'Toodle pip for now then, see you at the game.' Mr Doolally made to go and then turned back. 'By the by, I've decided to change the venue.'

'What?' spluttered Woolly in astonishment.

'No need to worry. I will make all the necessary arrangements. I thought it would be just splendid to play at the Cricket Club of India when the England side plays. You know, make a bit more of an event of it.'

'But that will make it an away fixture, and we were going to play at home.'

'Is that really going to make a difference? Oh dear, Woolly wants to play on his 'ickle cwicket pitch,' Doolally said, putting on a babyish voice.

'Have it your own way,' Woolly conceded.

'Good, that's settled. My man will pick you all up and take you there.'

Mr Doolally and his henchman skittered away and disappeared through a hole in the plaster.

Beaky, whose attitude to life had changed somewhat with his travels, had been watching from a distance. His sense of outrage at the various injustices it appeared Mr Doolally was responsible for made his blood boil. Without hesitation, as Doolally disappeared, Beaky set off in pursuit.

Outside the building, Mr Doolally's chauffeur was waiting to collect them. He had positioned the wicker cage over the hole they'd entered the building through. As his passengers emerged into the outside world, he watched them hop into it one by one before closing its door, sealing them safely inside. He'd just started to lift it as Beaky emerged into the sunlight. From dark to light, it took a moment for his eyes to adjust. He was aware of the shadowy form of the cage rising above him and leapt blindly at it. As he soared upwards, his flailing paws latching on to one of the wicker stands. He gritted his teeth and hung on, dangling precariously as the chauffeur returned to the tuk tuk. Once on the back seat, Beaky was able to scurry into a corner and squirm his way between the seat cushions to avoid detection.

Beaky stared out from his hiding place. The driver's back rose above him, twisting this way and that as he wove his way through the Mumbai traffic. How had, this man come to be working for a mouse?

Bhuman had been eking out a living as a litter picker and sleeping in the Chhatrapati Shivaji Railway Terminus. He'd roll his bedding up each morning after sleeping on the floor of the cathedral-like building. One morning, he'd woken to find a mouse curled up beside him. At first, the mouse had been wary of his new companion, scuttling away as the station came to life. However, day after day, the bond between them grew until the mouse was happy to be handled by his human friend.

Their business opportunity had presented itself in the form of a slightly mouldy piece of cheese Bhuman had found one day. That evening, he'd given his mouse friend a lump of it. The next morning, he'd woken to find the mouse sleeping on a ten-rupee note. It was as if the tooth fairy had become the cheese fairy. The next fragment brought more money, and soon the problem became where the cheese would come from rather than how they'd distribute it. So the business snowballed. The days of the station life behind them, premises were rented and a fridge purchased. The tuk tuk was next on the shopping list, and with the extra mobility, their business went from strength to strength.

The only problem with the business was that it was due to the mouse's contacts that it thrived. Bhuman gradually went from equal partner to 'gofer', running all over the city while the self-styled Mr Doolally presided over the empire.

Between them, they'd developed a series of directions using a free tourist pamphlet available at the station. In time, Bhuman had added to the pictures, and by now it was a grimy and slightly ragged document.

The well-worn route back to Chor Bazaar needed no prompting and Bhuman made good progress through the traffic. Twenty minutes later, the tuk tuk was parked at Supreme Motors, with whom Bhuman had an arrangement. It was better to walk the short distance than try to negotiate the vehicle through the crowded market.

Beaky, sensing their ride was at an end, ventured out of his hiding place and clung to the back of the cage. Bhuman reached into the back of the tuk tuk and slipped the velvet cover over the cage before lifting it off the back seat.

In the cellar of the Bombay Yacht Club, Beaky had now been missed. Feelings were mixed at the discovery. Compo and Bumble feared for their friend's safety, whilst Uncle was relieved that Bhoo had an ally. They all took comfort from the fact that there was no way Doolally would miss the cricket match. Hopefully, he'd hand Bhoo back after the game unless he intended to play him. If that had been his idea, then he'd shot himself in the foot by enlisting Bashar. Bashar, having stoked the rivalry between them, had created an impossible pairing. A problem that Woolly had sought to resolve by dropping Bashar and which now Mr Doolally had given himself.

Back at Chor Bazaar, the dark interior of *Cricket Curios* was brought to life by the flick of the ancient Bakelite switch. A radio, wired into a light socket, also crackled to life. Bhuman drew back the heavy curtain at the back of the shop and revealed the dusty, ancient Rolls Royce sitting imperiously at the back of the shop. Inside it he set down the wicker cage and opened its door. Mr Doolally strode out of it importantly and opened a concealed compartment with the twist of a knob. What had been a drinks cabinet now provided a mirror-walled 'super mouse dwelling'.

'Hello, my little friend. How are we bearing up this morning?' he enquired of Bhoo, who'd been shut inside the compartment.

'May I go home now please, sir?' Bhoo replied shakily.

'Home? But you've barely arrived, dear boy. No, no, no, it's certainly not time to go home yet. Anyway, I've brought a friend to keep you company. You know Bashar I believe.'

Bhoo shrank back in horror.

'There's no need to be frightened; we're all on the same side,' Doolally explained. 'Isn't that right, Bashar?'

Bashar nodded grumpily.

'Come on, Bashar, play nicely with Bhupathi,' Doolally scolded Bashar like a naughty child. 'We're all going to get along famously and win that lovely cup. For now, I'm afraid you're going to have to enjoy your own company for just a little while longer.'

Beaky hadn't thought his rescue plan through but decided now was the time to act. He leapt from his hiding place with a cry of 'HAA!', his two front paws stretched out karate style. Unfortunately, he'd tripped over his tail at the crucial moment, allowing Bashar to immobilise him simply by putting his foot on the back of his neck.

'A visitor,' Mr Doolally clapped his paws in delight. 'How lovely for you, Bhoo, to have some company. Mohit, Rohit, secure him.' Mr Doolally's tone suddenly became gruff and business-like. Beaky struggled, but he was no match for Doolally's henchmen, who'd travelled with him. Together they swept him up and crammed him into a drawer in the cabinet.

At the front of the shop, the radio blared from a cluttered shelf. Bhuman was checking messages on his phone and listening with half an ear.

*'Very exciting news about our quest to find a suitable trophy for this weekend's Bombay Brother's Match. A listener has sent in a drawing of the actually trophy. I have the picture right in front of me on my screen. A little wooden elephant standing on an oval base... and two words, yes words, carved round it. Let me see, B-O-M-B –a-y—D-u-c-k,'* he spelt out the lettering. *'There you have it, the Bombay Duck Trophy. I'm sure that there is someone out there who can either find or make us a trophy that fits that description, jaldi chalo!'*

Bhuman had a call to make. His conversation was monosyllabic, punctuated with the odd 'haan, ji or acha.' As he cradled the phone under his chin, he idly rummaged through the items of bric-a-brac on the dusty shelf in front of him. A pocket watch, a huge old padlock, an ink-stained printing block. A bowl of doorknobs, a compass with an old dented brass case, an elephant bell and a little wooden elephant to go with it. A little wooden elephant, precisely what the DJ had described. Bhuman picked it up and turned it over in his fingers. On the base, some roughly carved letters, difficult to make out at first, but with aid of a licked finger, they were legible... and spelt out the words the announcer had described, B-O-M-B-a-y D-U-C-K.

Over the next few hours, the offices of the radio studio were inundated with deliveries of elephants of every shape and sort. Each one carved, painted, glued with the words 'Bombay Duck Trophy.' It was an overwhelming response, and soon the DJ was pleading with his listening public, broadcasting that they had enough and would people kindly stop. However, one detail he failed to mention was how the words were written.

The tinkling of a bell signalled that Doolally needed his sidekick. In the back of the car, he found that he'd climbed back into the cage with Bashar and was waiting to be transported. Bhuman put down the little elephant he was holding and sealed the cage door. He placed the cover over the cage, and the party left the shop on their way to their next port of call.

In the darkened shop on the floor of the Rolls Royce sat the little carved elephant. In its long history, it had spent much of its time lost or discarded, this was just another chapter.

Inside Doolally's home, Beaky called out, 'Is there anybody there? Hello?'

'Yes,' squeaked Bhoo.

'Any chance you could get me out of here?' Beaky asked.

'But what if the others come back? They'll be cross with me.' Bhoo was reluctant to go to his aid.

'I know you're frightened, a long way from home and separated from those that you love, but I am too. We'll be stronger together, you and I, you'll see. So be a good fellow and give this drawer a good hard pull.'

Bhoo was in a quandary. Life had moved on quite quickly in the last few days. He'd rarely had to worry about anything other than playing cricket and keeping his whiskers clean before now. In a matter of days, he'd left home, achieved his cricketing dream, been kidnapped, and now he found himself having to go up against gangsters… what did he have to lose?

## Chapter Twelve

A message on his voicemail had summoned Assistant Station Master Moti Kumar to the offices of the Senior Divisional Operations Manager of the railway. It was with a certain degree of trepidation that Moti entered the oldest part of Chhatrapati Shivaji Railway Station. He made his way, as instructed, to an area off limits to the general public. Moti entered through an old pair of double doors and found himself beneath the building's main dome.

'May I help you?' a man in a dated military style uniform enquired. He was seated at a dark wooden writing desk with a clipboard in front of him.

'Good day to you, I'm required to visit the office of the Senior Divisional Operations Manager,' replied Moti.

'Name please?'

'Moti Kumar, that is Assistant Station Master Moti Kumar.' He squared his shoulders and stood as straight as he could to appear more important. The information initiated the rummaging through of many pages fastened to the clipboard.

'You are to see the Assistant to the Assistant of the Senior

Divisional Operations Manager. Follow the grand staircase up until you come to a set of iron spiral stairs. At the top of that, you will find his office, 19A,' the paper shuffler ordered.

Moti did as he was told and followed the splendid winding staircase up to the second floor. There, on a balcony open to the elements, he found the old wrought iron spiral staircase. At the top of it, he discovered a cylindrical office with 19A on the door.

'Please come in,' came the reply to his tentative knock. 'Ah, Mr Kumar, I've been expecting you,' Jignesh Patel, the Assistant to the Assistant of the Senior Divisional Operations Manager, grinned broadly. He appeared to be walled in behind heaps of stuffed, fawn-coloured binders, each bound with string. Moti eyed them nervously.

'So much paperwork,' Jignesh responded to Moti's unspoken question and scratched the side of his head vigorously.

'I received a message,' Moti ventured, trying to get the conversation back on track.

'Yes indeed, good news, Mr Kumar. I have the pleasure to inform that you did rather well in the Annual Training and Assessment course. In fact, you were top of the class.'

'Oh my, that is a surprise, err... I mean, obviously I pride myself on an in-depth knowledge of Railway Practice. I was worried that my being summoned meant bad news.'

'Not at all, not at all, not at all.' Mr Patel did a passable impersonation of the Pushpak Express train. 'It is my honour to extend to you an invitation to open the new upgrade to the Terminal's Train Management System. On Saturday morning, you are to attend a short ceremony in the Control Room to unveil the new twelve-metre long LED screen. This update to the system will mean that every train over the 53 kilometres of train lines in Mumbai can be seen at any one time.'

'Saturday morning,' Moti replied blankly. It wasn't as if his diary was overflowing with invitations, but now he had two that clashed.

'What an honour, don't you agree?'

'Yes, a great honour, thank you.' Moti endeavoured to maintain his composure whilst experiencing the most excruciating inner turmoil.

'Remember to wear your full uniform for the camera,' Mr Patel said brightly. 'Now if you'll forgive me, I must get back to… this,' he said, indicating the mounds of paperwork on his desk.

Moti struggled to comprehend the mixture of good and bad fortune fate had dealt him. Going in the opposite way that he needed to go, he left the building and wandered out into the road in a trancelike funk.

At that precise moment, Mr Doolally's Dalmatian-spotted tuk tuk whizzed by, and Bhuman leant on its shrill horn. The tuk tuk's raspy horn produced a sound like a strangled goat and the prolonged BLLLLLURRHGGGGGHHH brought Moti to his senses. He deftly sidestepped the vehicle and watched it disappear down the road in a fog of blue exhaust. He looked at his watch. *My goodness, they'll be missing me at the station*, he thought to himself, and with that, he dashed back into the terminal to hop on a train back to Mahim Junction.

As Moti caught his train, Mr Doolally's tuk tuk was pulling into the leafy tree lined Dinshaw Vacha Road on its way to Brabourne Stadium. At the gate, Bhuman managed to talk his way in, using the delivery of the package on the seat behind him as an excuse. Soon he was parked amongst the other vehicles in front of the art deco clubhouse and pavilion of the Cricket Club of India. Even Mr Doolally with his connections couldn't just stroll in through the front doors of the Cricket Club of India, so Bhuman sidled up to the building just to the left of them.

Here thick ivy grew up the wall, which, as he crouched beside it, provided good cover. He lifted one side of a plastic plate, hinged by one remaining screw in the top left corner. It appeared to have three cricket stumps embossed on it. In fact, the three stumps were the logo of III, India Internet Incorporated. It had been fitted when the club had taken a leap into the 21$^{st}$ century. Fibre optic cable had been installed to keep it in line with the technological demands of broadcasting agencies. Unwittingly, the club had also installed a super-fast mouse highway to the top of one of its iconic cylindrical towers.

Behind the building lay the playing surface, and from there, as with the Lord's Pavilion in London, one got the full effect of the building's design. It was intended to have a nautical look, whitewashed and complete with the odd porthole. At each end of the clubhouse stood two towers, each topped by rounded tent-like pediments. Similar in effect to the symmetrical turrets of the pavilion at Lord's Cricket Ground. But it was the cross between a saucer and a squashed dome shape at the top that the mice were interested in. On the outside, it supported a flagpole, the shape tapering up to a pleasingly decorative end. On the inside, it provided the perfect setting for a mouse cricket final. An ideal arena as though built for the purpose. The playing area was an exact circle lit by shafts of harsh Mumbai sun that poured in through a series of ventilation slots.

Mr Doolally and his entourage made their way up through the recently installed ducting, which provided a spiral walkway. In no time, they popped out onto the high-rise playing area. Preparations had been made for the forthcoming game, and Mr Doolally was pleased with what he saw.

'This looks very splendid,' he said to the team coach, who'd jogged over as soon as he saw his boss. Babs, or more correctly 'Baby', was the son of a cricketing colossus of the mouse cricketing world, Dinkar Kaplinkar. Dinkar had proudly named his son after himself, and so they'd been 'Daddy' Dinkar and 'Baby' Dinkar, and the name had stuck.

'I'm glad you like it. I think the shamianas are a nice touch,'

Around the boundary, brightly coloured tent-like shelters had been erected for the two teams and visiting supporters.

'The scoreboard is particularly smart,' Doolally remarked.

'Oh yes, we're particularly proud of that,' Baby remarked. 'It was quite a messy business, but worth the effort.'

The scoreboard had been painted with geometric and floral patterns in a rainbow of beautiful colours. Tell-tale splashes suggested that not all the paint had made it to its intended destination. However, it was a great centrepiece, with pins hammered into it on which to hang the scoring numbers.

The members of Doolally's team were going through a series of cricket related activities around the pitch.

'Hey, Baby, let's get those boys over here; I'd like to get to meet some of them. Give them a pep talk, gee them up, you know.'

Dinkar Junior, Baby, Babs, whatever it was he liked to be called, winced. It was not so much the order but the way it was phrased.

'Sure,' he replied casually, hiding his annoyance, before calling the players over.

It might seem strange that Mr Doolally as the manager of the team needed to be introduced to his players. The fact was that The Mumbai Cricketeers wasn't so much a team as an assortment of talented players whom Doolally had heard about. He'd begged, borrowed and stolen the talent of other local teams as a means to an end. To win the area title and cup at all costs.

Baby had the players line up and then walked Mr Doolally down the line, introducing the players as if he was the King of Mumbai.

'So first we have our captain, Tiger. He's a batsman of the highest order. He's also an inspirational leader, able to instil the belief in winning to his fellow players.'

'Excellent, pleased to have you on board,' Mr Doolally said smarmily.

'Bashar, you know better than most. A destructive batsman who has punished us in the past, so we're pleased to have him on our side this time.'

'I thought I was going to be the captain,' Bashar barked ungraciously.

'You won't go unrewarded, I assure you,' Doolally placated him.

'Now to the first of our pace bowlers. This is Bhuvi. He can be quite nippy with the new ball. He has a good away swinger and then one that cuts back in. So you can imagine, he can be quite a handful.'

'Hmm... good, good,' Doolally pronounced thoughtfully.

'Vishy is a true artist with the willow. His strokeplay, particularly the late-cut, is nothing less than divine. He is equally adept against pace and spin with his twinkling footwork.' Baby spoke fondly of the diminutive mouse in front of him.

'Who is this handsome fellow?' Doolally asked of the next character in the line, who had big black bushy whiskers.

'This is Rookie, he is our wicketkeeper, one of the best of his trade and a decent bat too. He likes to get stuck into the opposition from ball one.'

Mr Doolally shook him by the paw and then ducked away as if dodging a boxer's punch. 'Don't get stuck into me, will you?' he joked, at which Rookie chuckled politely.

'What do you think so far?' Baby asked.

'Shabash!' exclaimed Doolally. 'Excellent, most excellent, who's next?'

'Zak here is our other quick bowler. He has that added nuisance factor of bowling left arm. I challenge you to find any right-handed batsman who likes facing left arm over the wicket.'

'And next we have Dev. He's our secret weapon because he bowls a fast out-swinger, an in-swinging yorker, a steepling bouncer and a back-of-the-hand mystery ball. Oh, and he can bat a bit too!'

'Aha, an all-rounder, eh? Yes, I remember you're one of the Wankhede Stadium mice. I had the devil's own job to prise you from there. Your coach was very possessive.'

'Was...?' asked Baby nervously.

'Don't fret, Baby.' This made all the players in the line laugh. 'He's just fine, and I hear he'll be leaving the veterinary hospital any day now.'

Baby looked horrified.

'I'm kidding, Baby!' The lined up players laughed again.

Baby motioned for Mr Doolally to step to one side. 'Do you think you could call me something else in front of the team?'

'Sure thing, Baby... oops, I mean Mr Baby.'

'"Coach", might be good,' Baby suggested.

'Gotcha again,' Doolally howled, clapping him on the back. 'Come on, let's see the last of them.'

'This is Jaddu,' Baby continued, trying to restore what was left of his dignity. 'A slow left-arm orthodox bowler and middle-order batsman.'

'Fine set of whiskers on you too,' observed Mr Doolally of Jaddu, who had the makings of a neat little beard on his chin.

'Gauti will open the batting with Bashar,' Baby introduced the next mouse in the line. 'As a left-hander, the combination with the right-handed Bashar will work well for us. His correct form will complement the more swashbuckling approach of his partner.'

'Next we have Shaz, who is a bit of an old hand. A slow left-arm bowler who'll bat anywhere, catch anything and is a useful player to have for the captain to consult.'

'What a fine bunch,' Doolally declared, rubbing his paws together.

Baby got them all back to work, and Mr Doolally watched their progress from the boundary. They were a fine collection of players in their own right, and the venue was splendid, but would it all come together? Mr Doolally and his team would find out soon enough, the next day.

Mr Doollaly

## Chapter Thirteen

After a day spent kicking about the Bombay Yacht Club ground, the feeling of helplessness had finally got the better of Compo and Bumble. They'd questioned Sunni about his acquaintance Jeet, and if he could lead them to Doolally's 'godown'. With the aid of a map on the back of a local car hire firm's business card, they'd planned the route to Chor Bazaar. On the map, the distance they were required to travel looked doable. However, that was in the compact world depicted on the back of the card and not in the real world.

'Realistically, how far do you think we can run?' Compo asked.

'I've run right across the Lord's pitch and back no problem,' boasted Bumble.

'Yes, but we've probably only got an hour's worth of puff, maybe an hour and a half, before we need a good rest and a feed.'

'Not if we take the rickshaw,' Sunni suggested. 'Then we can take it in turns to pedal, and we will make much faster progress on three wheels.'

'But the rickshaw will make us a big target for anything and everything. Goodness knows we have enough predators as it is,' Compo reasoned.

'I don't know, there are a lot of culverts and open drains in Mumbai to deal with the monsoon rains we can use. We may have to manhandle the rickshaw at times, but if we're creative with our route, we should make it. Let's see how heavy it is for the three of us.'

The three mice went over to Sunni's rickshaw and lifted it between them.

'Phew, it's a bit awkward, but not too heavy,' Sunni said, as they lowered it back to the ground.

'I vote we don't do too much lifting, my creaking back will be giving me jip.'

'That's fine, Bumble, you can just sit in the back with your feet up,' Compo remarked irritably.

'I'll do my bit, never you mind, son.' There was an edge to Bumble's tone. It was unlike him to be chippy, which suggested he was perhaps having second thoughts about the trip.

'I'm sure he will,' Sunni added, smoothing things over.

Bumble was right to be concerned. Even with the most carefully drawn up plan, back-up crew and supplies, it would be tricky. This, however, was a spur of the moment thing. Half-baked, hare-brained, there were many ways to describe it. Whilst also being well intentioned and selfless to the point, that ultimately, they were putting their lives on the line for their friends.

With a rough plan of the route and a hastily written note to Woolly left pinned to the scoreboard that read.

*'Woolly, have gone to rescue Bhoo and Beaky.*
*See you at the cricket tomorrow one way or another.*
*Love Sunni'*

They set off following the route that Doolally and his henchman had taken. It led them from the cellar of the old Yacht Club to the outside world and Mumbai's after-dark world.

Soon Ayesha and Woolly were poring over the note.

'Oh my goodness, we must get after them. Who knows what will become of them if Doolally's sidekicks get hold of them.' Woolly's face was a picture of concern.

'I think that's the least of their problems.' Ayesha's anxious look spoke volumes. 'There are a lot of hungry mouths on the Mumbai streets after dark. I doubt they'll get that far.'

Woolly whipped up some of the others to try and stop them, but it was already too late—there was no sign of them.

Geographically speaking, the three friends were still quite nearby. They'd had a smooth passage through the leafy surroundings of the old club. During the day, there was more activity here because of its close proximity to the tourist attraction the Gateway to India. But hawkers and street food vendors attracted all sorts of scavengers, and they were relieved to bump down the broken edge of an open drain. Here they made good progress, running along behind the hotel that housed Gogi's bookshop and the England team. Their first dead-end required them to put their lifting expertise to the test. Sunni jumped up onto the handlebars. From there he was able to jump up to the street level. Bumble and Compo did their best to lift up the front wheel while Sunni leaned over the edge of the pavement and grabbed it. With him pulling and them pushing, they were able to negotiate their first major obstacle.

They found themselves on a side road, and they crossed it with ease. Light poured from the open-fronted 'Pretty Boy' barbershop, spilling onto and lighting their path. The barber was just executing an intricate trim round the ear of his client as the mouse-powered rickshaw rattled past. Momentarily distracted, he caught the fleshy lobe, sparking an altercation with the snipped client. As he two men flapped at each other, the mice made their way down the path and turned into the main drag of Colaba Causeway.

The side of the road they were on was lined with stalls selling everything and anything one could imagine.

'How are you doing? Do you need a break yet?' asked Compo.

'Not too bad,' puffed Sunni. 'I'll keep going for a bit. I reckon our best bet is to try and use the shoppers as cover. I'll do my best to weave between them, and hopefully we'll find a place to cross farther down.'

'I better hold on to me 'at!' Bumble cried as they lurched off towards the busy market area.

A stall selling electronic goods had the radio on, from it the local newscaster reported.

*'After an exciting build up, it is the eve of the commemorative match taking place at the Cricket Club of India's Brabourne ground tomorrow. After a drive, championed by this station, to find a worthwhile way to celebrate this great event. I'm pleased to say that I'm joined by Mr Ram Verma of Holistic Holi Powders Ltd. Good evening, sir.'*

*'Good evening. It's great to be with you.'*

*'That's a relief, I thought you were going to turn me purple,'* the newscaster joked.

'It can be arranged,' Mr Verma joked back.

'Tell me, what is it you have planned for us?'

'We at Holistic Holi Powders are much taken with the story of the Bombay Brothers. Since we are normally associated with the "festival of sharing love", it seemed like an excellent fit. So we'll be awarding a trophy, provided by our friends at Trophy Corner *of Crawford Market*, and arranging for a bit of local colour as well.'

'Thank you, Mr Verma, we'll look forward to tomorrow. There we must leave it,' the newscaster cut his guest off and moved onto the next item.

Progress under the tables of stallholders was easier than the intrepid mice had expected. Eventually, however, this safe thoroughfare came to an end. A concrete municipal refuse area provided an unexpected hazard. Above it on a telephone sat a line of sleepy crows. Up to now, they'd been fortunate in avoiding the unwanted attention the rattle of the rickshaw attracted. But now one of the bird's cocked an eye open. Attracted by the light glinting off the rickshaw's chrome, it swooped down and fluttered about the mice.

'IN-COMING!' Bumble shouted.

The crow fluttered about, pecking at the two friends in the back in a flurry of coarse, waxy, wing beats. In an attempt to outrun their assailant, Sunni put his head down and pedalled for all he was worth.

Bumble took his hat off and attempted to bat the bird away as it did its best to peck at the top of his head.

'Hey, geroff me!' he yelled. The crow replied with a flurry of attacks. Compo did his best to lend a hand and flapped at it energetically. But the bird was determined and strong. It wasn't going to give up on the opportunity of a meal on wheels easily. Finally, the tuft of fur the bird had a grip of parted company with Bumble's head.

'YEEOOOW!' Bumble cried.

The crow faltered for an instant, then renewed its attack. Sunni had seen a drainage pipe ahead. Without hesitation, he hauled on the handlebars and plunged down it and into darkness. They'd made it in the nick of time. It had the double effect of warding off their attacker and transporting them safely across the busy road.

'Oooh, he nearly got me.' Bumble sat back heavily in the rear seat in relief.

'Nonsense,' Sunni called over his shoulder. 'It wasn't even close.'

'Yer what? He pecked the top of me 'ead off!'

'He'd need a bigger beak for that,' Sunni joked back, and

the friends' laughter echoed down the pipe. It was a good place to have a change of driver. Sunni brought them to a halt, and Compo hopped up onto the saddle. Grimacing in the darkness, he pushed the pedal round and eased the rickshaw out of the pipe and back out onto the street.

'Where to now?' he asked.

'We need to be going that way.' Sunni pointed in a direction that corresponded to the number two on a clock face. He was right, but their journey from here was far from straightforward. They pressed on for the next hour, climbing, pushing and pedalling. Dodging unmarked holes in the ground. Ducking under overhanging hazards. Squeezing their vehicle through small gaps and diving for cover when the need arose. Bumble took over the driving and the relentless slog continued. Too far from home to turn back but with an uncertain passage ahead.

Elsewhere, the build up to the following day continued. In London, Joe Wilson, the BBC's sports correspondent, made a report to camera for the afternoon news. It was broadcast with the Grace Gates of Lord's Cricket Ground as his backdrop.

'The England tour of India gets underway tomorrow with an exhibition match in the city of Mumbai, a curtain-raiser for the *forthcoming series. There's a historic background for this head to head...'* the reporter fleshed out the story.

*'A tour of the subcontinent brings with it its own particular challenges. Even those with experience of India will find the combination of local conditions hard to overcome. Extreme heat, dry dusty pitches that will suit the Indian spinners and the sheer weight of support are things to which they'll have to adapt. Everywhere they go will be packed with passionate and knowledgeable cricket fans, all of them keen to see how they'll fare against one of the best teams in the world. From Mumbai, they head to Dharamsala, one of the most picturesque grounds in the world, with its scenic backdrop of the Himalayas. A final warm-up game before the first Test in Kolkata in a weeks' time.'*

The reporter was certainly right about the weight of numbers. The Centenary Game was a sell-out. On top of the numbers inside the stadium, there would still be hundreds trying to get in. For now, the streets were clearing. For the most part, Mumbaikars all over the city were resting up at home after their busy day. Those less fortunate and for whom the streets were home did their best to find what comfort they could. One of those, a skinny goat inexplicably left tied to some railings, was just starting to waver on his feet as sleep overcame him. At this moment, the mouse-powered rickshaw, with Bumble at the helm, whirred below him as if he were a bridge. The startled goat let out a tremulous bleat, which in turn stirred a group of three pye-dogs sleeping in a huddle on the other side of the railings.

Whatever it was that sped past on other side of the railings was definitely of interest. In the minds of the dogs, that meant it was worth chasing, and they shot off in hot pursuit. The dogs, it seemed, had gone from nought to warp speed in a matter of seconds. Fortunately for the mice, the railings kept them at bay and the two groups ran side by side.

'Oh heck, I'm not going to be able to outrun them,' Bumble wailed.

Sunni and Compo were on their feet in the back of the rickshaw.

'You can do it, Bumble!' they shouted in unison, urging him on like a pair of jockeys. But Bumble, who was out of the saddle dancing on the pedals for all he was worth, was running out of puff. A gap in the railings ahead would surely bring an abrupt end to their journey.

As he looked to his left and saw the dogs side by side with them, he hoped the end, when it came, would be quick.

They arrived at the gap, and the dogs poured through it, overshooting their quarry wildly, while Bumble pulled hard down left on the handlebars. For an instant, the two groups swapped sides of the railings. The surface was flat and sandy and a slight downward slope gave the rickshaw new momentum. The dogs made their turn and gave chase once again. Poor Bumble was really flagging now.

'Come on, Bumble! One last push!' Compo urged.

'Over there!' Sunni cried, pointing to a tree, its roots forming a v-shaped garage for the rickshaw. Bumble did as he was told and plunged headlong towards the gap. Perhaps some other furry quarry had had cause to take refuge here. They found that the sandy soil had been hollowed out, giving them just enough space to stow the rickshaw, skip out of it and use it as a barricade between them and the dogs. For a moment, the dogs lost them, they'd been too smart for them. They loped blindly in their general direction without focus, but soon they rallied and circled the tree, sniffing at its base.

'Sit tight, they'll soon get bored,' Sunni instructed the others.

At that moment, a battle-scarred snout was thrust into the hollow and sniffed and snorted about it.

'Oooer, they don't seem to be losing interest,' whimpered Bumble.

'Oh aren't they,' said Sunni boldly. 'Let's see if this puts a different complexion on things.' With that, he squirmed his way under the rickshaw until he was right up against the dog's nose. Once in place, he clamped his teeth into it as firmly as he could.

The dog let out a fearsome yelp and withdrew its nose as if it had received an electric shock. The sudden movement took Sunni by surprise, and for an instant, still attached, he found himself in the night air. The dog shook its head and Sunni lost his grip and fell to the ground. There he lay for a moment, stunned.

The dog buried his snout in the ground and put both his paws on it to soothe it. As he did so, he spotted his assailant in front of him. The other two dogs edged up to join him, and for a moment, all three of them hovered over the defenceless furry form. A large globule of saliva ran from the lead dog's mouth and plopped on Sunni's head. But the saying goes 'you snooze you lose', and it would seem they'd snoozed. In an instant, Compo and Bumble sped out of their hiding place and dragged their friend back to safety. The dogs stood in shocked disbelief for a moment before resuming their snarling and sniffing about the friends' hiding place.

'What happened to me?' asked Sunni as he regained consciousness.

'Flying in the face of danger, quite literally,' replied Bumble with a smirk.

Compo had a more measured response, 'I think we've all had quite enough excitement for one evening, and we should sit tight till morning.'

## Chapter Fourteen

Gogi Singh could not believe his luck. For years, his scooter had proved a reliable, if not sensational, mode of transport. Now, when he needed it most, it failed him. Wearing his best suit, with an eye on his watch, he jogged to the local station, again not something to which he was accustomed. Despite it being a Saturday, the train was still crowded. His ticket only guaranteed him a seat on the train if he was prepared to work for it. In the end, he'd decided to go for a different form of comfort, preferring to enjoy the breeze that standing in the space between the doors afforded.

Moti Kumar had travelled in on the train too. The spanner in the works of his day had been inserted by his own hard work and efficiency. As long as things ran to schedule, he'd be able to cut the ribbon on, smash the bottle of Sula Fizz against, or whatever you use to open a new twelve-metre-long LED screen.

Bhuman had plans for later in the day too. Before that, he'd have to complete his chores. These involved the ferrying around of the various parties taking place in the area title match between the two teams of mice.

He was aware that there were a lot of moving parts to his day, namely eleven players and their many supporters. Things had not started well. There had been an unsettling scene in the shop when the time had come to take Bhupathi from the back of the Rolls Royce.

'If Beaky doesn't go, I won't go,' he stated defiantly, clinging to the lining of his prison. The young mouse, despite his determination, was no match for Doolally's henchman, who prised his claws off it painfully.

Beaky called out from inside his drawer, 'Don't worry about me! Take care of yourself.'

Beaky had plans of his own, which didn't include hanging around. As such, he'd been hard at work gnawing an escape route out of the old car. Once he'd got through the hard wood of the cabinet, the faded, decaying fabric of the vehicle had been pretty easy to chomp his way through. In fact, unknown to his jailers, he'd already been able to venture out. He'd encountered the little wooden elephant figure on the floor of the back of the car. In the shadows, the encounter had at first freaked him out. But once he'd found him to be made of wood, he'd quite enjoyed having him for company.

So Bhuman's first port of call had been to drop Mr Doolally,

Bhoo and his minders off at the Cricket Club of India's Brabourne Stadium. Bhoo would need persuading that playing was in his best interest and would need a run out with the rest of the team. The England team and their opposition for the Centenary Game had done likewise. They were out on the playing surface taking part in the various warm-up drills and pre-match practice that is required of international cricketers.

In the meantime, Bhuman set off to collect the opposition and their supporters from the Bombay Yacht Club. Woolly had got his team together, or rather what was left of it. With Bhoo's absence, Sunni, as twelfth man, was the obvious replacement, but he too was missing. If only the three English cricketers hadn't all managed to get themselves lost, he might have been able to call on one them. In a worst-case scenario, he'd play himself, but perhaps Doolally would relent in the name of sportsmanship and hand Bhoo over.

The mice had assembled by the hole to the outside world, awaiting collection. The girls had dressed in their finest, and the cricketers had all their kit with them. Woolly, Uncle and Mr Googly waited patiently at the back of the line. A lookout peered out onto the busy area outside. There was still no sign of Doolally's driver. There were so many drivers parked up due to the proximity of the large international hotel and the Gateway to India that he was struggling to get near enough to stop. Street vendors and hawkers, little kids, the odd snake charmer and a pigeon population attracted by the comings and goings of the many tourists made venturing out to find him impossible. Bhuman was anxious to get going too, as he had an appointment of his own to keep. Eventually, a parking space opened up and Bhuman swooped into it. The collection of the waiting mice was made in a stop that would have made a Formula One team proud. In no time, the Dalmatian-spotted vehicle was back on the road with its passengers on board.

At the stadium, the sweet-talking of the gateman was getting harder with each visit. He was particularly twitchy on account of all the VIPs due to make an appearance. Reluctantly, he let the tuk tuk and its driver into the car park, and Bhuman was able to discharge his passengers. He ushered them from the wicker cage through the plastic plate. Here they were met and escorted up the spiral ducting to the turret top cricket ground.

Back in the cab of the tuk tuk, Bhuman took a small piece of towel from his pocket and wiped his face. Despite all his running around, it was only now that he was beginning to sweat. He made a call on his cell phone.

'See you there in 30 minutes, don't be late,' he said abruptly into the handset before engaging the clutch and roaring off into the traffic again.

At the top of the turret, the mice from the Yacht Club spilled onto the playing surface.

'Oh my goodness, this is pretty spectacular,' Ayesha trilled, doing a pirouette.

'Hrmmmpf,' said Woolly in response. 'We'll see.' He prodded the ground suspiciously with his toe.

Bhoo, who was on the other side of the ground, couldn't believe his eyes. 'Hey, everybody, I'm here, Uncle! Woolly! Everyone!' he cried.

'Restrain him,' Doolally ordered coolly to his sidekicks before sauntering over to greet the visitors.

'So glad you could make it to my little place,' the master manipulator said, grinning from ear to ear and making an expansive gesture with his arm.

'Let me see my nephew, you rotter,' demanded Uncle, pushing his way through the group.

'Yes, we want our 2½-inch run machine,' the others cried.

'He's playing for us. Of course, I'm sure you'd already gathered that. Anyway, I'm not sure he wants to see you right now,' Doolally announced, throwing the comment into the air with delight, knowing the storm it would provoke. As he spoke, Bhoo was grabbed roughly and bundled out of sight.

'Why you devil!' Woolly struggled to get at the smug little creature.

'Woolly, no!' Mr Googly ordered.

Woolly stopped in his tracks, muttering to himself and punching his fist into the palm of his hand in frustration.

'It is too late. If the boy has been persuaded or forced to play and is now against us, then there is nothing we can do. We must simply accept that fact and play the game in the spirit in which we believe.'

The travelling mice let out a collective, 'NOOOOO!' to which Mr Googly held up a restraining paw.

Now that Bhoo was out of sight, it seemed that what Doolally was telling them was indeed true. There was nothing else they could do but knuckle down and hope they could take their revenge on the pitch.

Elsewhere, Gogi's Western Line train was approaching Chhatrapati Shivaji Terminus. He eased his way to the doors as the train pulled into the station. Some intrepid souls would step from it whilst it was still moving. He'd give that a miss. But as soon as the train was stationary, he was on the platform running as fast as he could.

Up above him, Moti was on the move too. He'd dislodged a sheet, the preferred method of unveiling the new train management system, and said his thank yous. Then having made his excuses, he'd hurtled out of the door and down the grand staircase and out through the double doors. Once on the street, Moti decided that the best course of action was to hail a taxi. An elderly Hindustan Ambassador was idling along the road, and Moti waved it down. At the same moment, Gogi arrived from the opposite direction with the same idea.

'This is my cab!' Gogi exclaimed. 'I need it.'

'No, I need it,' Moti countered.

'I have an urgent appointment at the Cricket Club of India, at Brabourne Stadium. I should have been there...' Gogi checked his watch, 'ten minutes ago!'

'Me too...' Moti stopped short before asking. 'Bombay Brothers?'

'Absolutely!' Gogi beamed.

'Well, hop in!'

The old Ambassador car made surprisingly fast progress to

the Brabourne Stadium. Having paid the taxi driver, both men armed themselves with their invitation cards and ran to the gate.

The gateman, who'd seen fit to let tuk tuk drivers in and out all morning, became suddenly overzealous in his examination of their credentials.

'You're invited as special guests you say.'

'Yes, we're expected and a little late, so if you could...' Moti explained.

'Why would you be coming late if you are expected?'

Gogi slapped his forehead in disbelief. 'This is Mumbai, everyone is late for everything!'

'Please wait.'

The gateman made a call on an elderly telephone. The response he received caused him to hold the handset away from his ear as he was told in no uncertain terms to usher in the guests.

Once inside the clubhouse, the VIPs were whisked through the building and out onto the playing area. Although outside the ground people were still filing in, there was already a good crowd, which brought the stadium to life. The players of the two teams stood lined up, ready to be introduced to the attending dignitaries. A small, brightly coloured military band, who'd been playing a rousing, but unrecognisable oom-pah-pah-type tune, marched away having finished their set. Between the two teams stood a small podium with a bulbous microphone on a stalk protruding from it. General Baig, an impressive-looking army officer with a chest full of medals, marched up to it and leant into it to speak.

'Good morning, ladies, gentleman, distinguished guests, boys and girls, welcome to Brabourne Stadium, the home of the Cricket Club of India.'

The crowd roared its approval. The army officer raised a gloved hand to both acknowledge and quieten them down.

'Today we are here to commemorate the centenary of the Bombay Brothers' cricket match that took place in France during the First World War.'

The crowd let out a collective 'OOOOH!'

'I'm delighted to say that we have three descendants of the Bombay Brothers here today, and I'd like to ask them to step forward. First, Colonel Kulkarni...' There was a pause while the old gentleman walked out unsteadily. He took his place to one side of the podium and waved to the crowd, who showed their appreciation.

'Next, Mr Gogi Singh...' Gogi walked out briskly and acknowledged his fellow Mumbaikers like a film star.

'...and Mr Moti Kumar.' Moti instantly became very self-conscious, stooped his shoulders and waved briefly to the assembled masses.

'The VIP party will now be introduced to the two teams. This will be followed by the toss, presided over by Colonel Kulkarni.'

The England captain stepped forward and acknowledged the visitors before leading them along the lined-up players of his team. A great many handshakes were followed by a great many more as the captain of the Invitational XI introduced his team.

'Now, if Colonel Kulkarni would like to make the toss.' The old boy acknowledged his cue, stepped up shakily and felt in his pocket for the crucial coin. Rather predictably, it took several attempts to locate the correct pocket. When the coin was finally found, the colonel struggled to steady it on is thumb to flick it into the air. Eventually, however, the coin made its revolutions, the England captain correctly called 'heads' and elected to bat.

At Chor Bazaar, Bhuman was having a bit of a struggle. The many telephone calls he'd been making related to the old Rolls Royce in Mr Doolally's shop. Of the many 'treasures' Doolally owned, it was the jewel in his crown of oddities, antiques and curios. How Doolally viewed it differed from the way dealers in classic cars around the world viewed it. To the mouse, it was the most palatial dwelling he could imagine. To the classic car market, it was a 1930 Rolls Royce Phantom II worth 30 lakhs, or 3 million rupees. That sort of money would be quite useful to Bhuman, freeing him of his subservience to the tyrannical mouse. He'd searched the Internet and found a dealer in California prepared to buy the car unseen. It would undergo a complete 'nut and bolt', they called it, restoration and live happily ever after in the dry American state.

It would be shipped there in a container from the docks, but getting it there was probably the trickiest part of the whole transaction. All the reputable companies wanted to charge far more than he was prepared to pay. Getting into Chor Bazaar and trying to negotiate the busy streets with a truck and a trailer and manhandling an elderly vehicle would take time and patience. Eventually, he'd hired a guy called Pradeep from a local garage who had a rusty trailer and a free morning. Fortunately for Bhuman, Mr Doolally had been quite pernickety about the upkeep of the vehicle. He was particularly proud of the 'white wall' gangster-style tyres he'd had fitted to it. Doubtless this would raise eyebrows in the world of vintage car connoisseurship, but as far as Bhuman was concerned, it meant it would roll easily.

He'd just finished clearing a path for it through the shop when his cell phone rang.

'I've backed the trailer as far down the street as I can. If you look out of the door, you will see me,' Pradeep instructed.

'Can't you get any closer?' Bhuman was dismayed to find that that the trailer was blocking the narrow street and attracting just the sort of attention he didn't want.

'No, sir,' came the disappointing reply.

Resigned to the fact that that was as good as it was going to get, Bhuman opened the shutter at the front of the building. Pradeep arrived to lend a shoulder. Having rocked the old car to get it rolling, and with Bhuman steering through an open window, they negotiated it out of the shop. The tightest of turns presented itself to them, and Bhuman pressed a couple of lads who were enjoying the spectacle to help them. In no time, the sport of vintage Rolls Royce pushing caught on. As more people helped out, Bhuman was able to jump behind the wheel. He steered a path down the narrow street and up the two folding ramps onto the car trailer. The car's handbrake applied, he had only to lock the shop up and his life would change course for good.

Sunni, Compo and Bumble were still hiding in the hole in their tree. The dogs had eventually lost interest and slunk off to find somewhere to snooze.

'Do you think it's safe to venture out?' Compo asked.

'We can't very well stay here forever,' Bumble remarked accurately but unhelpfully.

Sunni crept out and had a look to see if the coast was clear. On a tree in front of him was a poster advertising the Bombay Brothers Centenary Game. It was a cool-looking poster made up of old photographs and more recent images. It was a mixture of soldiers from days gone by, archive cricket photos and more modern pictures given a sepia-style aged appearance. Sunni popped back into the hollow.

'Yes, we should make a move, but I think we are seriously lost, guys. It's all my fault I'm afraid, it seems I overestimated my sense of direction.' Sunni looked downcast.

'Maybe if we get going, you'll recognise where we are,' Compo said optimistically.

So they set off with Sunni back on the pedals. They passed through the gap in the railings and followed the road again.

The mice were not the only ones having trouble with their radar. Pradeep, having taken the job, found himself in a part of the city of which he had no knowledge. He was no expert at towing a trailer either, and in coping with it, he'd missed the road for the docks. Now he was doubling back on himself, retracing his route. On top of this, his trailer was old and rusty and in far from tip-top condition. He drove past the mice, who were beetling along the sidewalk as fast as Sunni could propel them. Up ahead of him, a set of traffic lights were turning red. For an instant, Pradeep was distracted by what appeared to be a child's toy rolling along the sidewalk. Then, eyes back on the road, the momentary distraction caused him to stand on the brakes. His truck screeched to a halt, the trailer slewed to one side and one of the ramps fell with a clatter, landing on the sidewalk. Sunni, head down and pedalling for all he was worth, failed to see it and drove straight up it.

Under the old car, the mice at first wondered why everything had gone dark. At that moment, up above them, Beaky spat out a fragment of wooden floor, creating a hole which he fell through. As if planned and rehearsed, he landed between Compo and Bumble in the rickshaw.

'What on earth...?' stuttered Bumble, who did a cartoon-style double take at the apparent magical reappearance of Beaky. Seconds later, he was further dumbfounded as a wooden elephant also appeared from nowhere, dropping from the heavens and narrowly missing Compo.

'Hello there, fancy meeting you here, hope you don't mind me bringing my little friend along,' Beaky said calmly, patting the elephant on the head.

'I've heard of it raining cats and dogs, but mice and elephants!' Bumble said, lifting his hat and scratching the top of his head in amazement.

Delighted to be reunited, the four mice high-fived each other.

'Now that we're all back together, we may as well sit tight and enjoy the ride,' Sunni observed, perched on the saddle with his feet on the handlebars. The friends sat back in the rickshaw while Beaky explained what had happened. Where they'd been imprisoned, and how Bhoo had been taken to the venue for the cricket match.

'That means he's at the Cricket Club of India, which means he's in the Brabourne Stadium, which is...' Sunni paused for a moment and his jaw dropped open. 'Which is right here,' he said dumbly.

The truck, still trailing the trailer's ramp, had come to a halt in traffic. They were right outside entrance to the Cricket Club of

India at the back of the stadium.

'WHAT?' bellowed Compo. 'Then, hit the gas.'

Sunni didn't hesitate, he dropped down onto the pedals and pulled a neat circle beneath the old Rolls Royce. His passengers held tight to the sides of the rickshaw. Beaky put an arm around his wooden friend, and they shot off down the ramp and in through the gates.

There was still plenty of activity at the main stadium entrance, but at the back of the pavilion and the entrance to the club, things had quietened down. The overworked gatekeeper was having a couple of minutes to himself. He'd ticked off all the names on the list he'd been issued that morning so felt he deserved a cup of chai and a biscuit. Sunni took full advantage of the coast being clear. With the elevated start from the ramp, the rickshaw sped under the barrier and the mice made their unscheduled arrival trouble free.

'Where to now?' Compo asked.

'They could be anywhere in the ground, right?' Beaky guessed.

'They could be, but it just so happens I know exactly where they are. Hold tight!' Sunni gritted his teeth and pressed on again.

## Chapter Fifteen

The Mumbai Mouse Cricket League Area Final

| **The Bombay Yacht Club Mouse XI** | **The Mumbai Cricketeers Invitational XI** |
|---|---|
| Bunni | Gauti |
| Gabbar | Bashar |
| Dervall | Tiger |
| Chiku | Vishy |
| Mahi | Shaz |
| Yoovi | Jaddu |
| Jumbo | Dev |
| Bhajji | Rookie |
| Lambu | Bhuvi |
| Ishy | Zak |

The twenty-over-a-side game between the Bombay Yacht Club and the Mumbai Cricketeers had got off to a bad-tempered start. With both teams counting on Bhoo to make up their eleven, one was going to be short.

'Our twelfth man has gone missing on account of you.' Woolly pointed an admonishing finger at Doolally. 'He went off to look for our batsman, who *you* kidnapped.'

'It has nothing to do with me, dear boy,' Doolally replied smugly. 'Anyway, the last time I counted, our team appeared to be all present and correct.'

'D'oh!' Woolly exploded. 'We've got our full team too. It just happens that one of the players is over there being detained against his will. He doesn't even have a bat. What good is *our* "run machine" to you without his bat?'

'We have plenty of bats for him. But okay, I tell you what we'll do. We'll share him.'

'What?'

'We won the toss, so he can bat for us first and then have a go for you,' Doolally suggested.

'That has never happened before in the history of cricket—one player playing for both sides—and it is not going to happen today,' Woolly snorted.

'There's always a first time for everything,' Doolally replied. 'But have it your own way then. He plays for us.'

Ayesha, who'd been listening to their squabble, put her paw on Woolly's arm.

'What harm can it do?'

'It just isn't cricket!' Woolly exclaimed.

'Well it won't be the sort of cricket we want to play if he's on the other side. If you don't say something now, then we'll lose him.'

Woolly moved away from her and considered her point.

'All right, Doolally, let Bhupathi play for both sides.'

There had been another clash over who would be the umpires. Doolally had suggested that they be his two henchmen. Again, this was an idea to which Woolly was firmly opposed.

'I could be an umpire,' Uncle had ventured.

With the complication of Bhoo playing for both sides, it was decided that this wasn't a good idea. Instead, it was decided that there would be no LBWs and those team members who were either out or who hadn't yet batted should umpire. So with all the little 'nit-picking' points resolved, the match finally got underway.

Below them, the rickshaw wallahs, Sunni, Beaky, Compo and Bumble, had arrived at the plastic plate. Sunni gave Compo a bunk up, and he scrambled through the opening and into the building. Bumble went next, Beaky followed him and then reached to help Sunni up.

'You guys go on ahead without me,' Sunni called up to him. 'You can make your own way; it's very straightforward. Follow the spiral up as far as you can go, and you'll find the game.'

'Where are you going?' asked Beaky.

'I'm going to take your little friend for one last ride.' He nodded in the direction of the wooden elephant. 'I'll see you later, theek hai!' With that, Sunni turned the rickshaw away from them and pedalled off.

'I'd grown quite attached to him,' Beaky said sadly.

'Awww, get away with you,' Bumble teased.

'Come on,' Compo urged. 'Let's find the others.'

Having lowered the plate, the mice found themselves in the spaceship-like surroundings of the aluminium foil ducting. Its wire, spiral skeleton provided an easy route to climb up, but the heat inside it was stifling.

'Phew, couldn't they have chosen somewhere more difficult to get to?' Bumble puffed sarcastically.

'Where's your sense of occasion?' Compo reasoned. 'I think it's pretty cool, listen to that...'

From the main stadium, the roar of the cricket-loving Mumbai public washed over them.

'Hear that, doesn't it remind you of home?' he said, cupping his paw to his ear.

A waft of fresher air signalled that their climb was at an end.

The little party scampered up the last few inches of ducting and burst out into the mouse cricketing arena.

'Would you look at that?' Bumble marvelled.

'That was worth the effort,' Beaky gushed.

Before them stretched the magnificent cricket ground Doolally had created. On the boundary was the scoreboard, a blank canvas on which the game would be mapped out. Under it stood the area trophy, and on either side of it were striped shamianas for the spectators. A good-natured collection from each side had gathered and waited expectantly for the action.

'Hold on a minute,' boomed Bumble, striding onto the pitch. 'Where's the umpire? You've got to have a proper, impartial umpire.'

Doolally sped out to join him. 'We don't have a proper umpire, now kindly move along.'

'You 'ave now. I'm even wearing me umpire's 'at. Now you skedaddle,' he said, pointing to the player officiating at the bowler's end. 'While you,' he pointed to the player in the square leg umpire's position, 'count to six, then swap with me.'

Everyone was rather taken aback by Bumble's forthright directions and complied meekly. Woolly did his best to hide a big grin that spread across his face.

'Righto, who's got the match ball?' Bumble demanded.

Doolally rolled it out to him, and Bumble picked it up.

'A very nice cherry,' he opined and lobbed it to Ishy, who was opening the bowling for the BYC. 'PLAY!' Bumble shouted, and the match began.

Ishy coolly pushed back his mane of black fur and shook a collection of ragged bracelets down his arm before running in to bowl the first ball. Gauti, receiving it, had taken his guard outside his crease to put the bowler off his length. The ploy didn't work, and in the end, he played an uncharacteristic hoick, nearly swinging himself off his feet in trying to over-hit it. He fared no better with the second, which kept low, and he missed it by a mile.

Bashar stood at the non-striker's end fuming. He'd played the opening over in his mind so many times, and it had certainly not gone this way. Finally, the scoreboard creaked into action when the next, a leg side ball, glanced Gauti's pad and Bashar barked that they run a bye. Mahi, who was both captain and wicketkeeper, came up to the stumps to stop Bashar using his 'dancing shoes' to move around the crease. This seemed to have the desired effect, producing two dot balls and a scampered single off the last ball of the over.

In his mind, at least, Bashar felt he had the upper hand, as he'd retained the strike. The opposition were wary of him—he'd go so far as to say frightened. If this was the case, Mahi wasn't showing it. He took the unconventional step of opening with spin at the other end.

Bhajji took the ball and spun the ball from hand to hand. Bashar licked his lips and the first ball of the over was bowled. Down the wicket Bashar strode and lofted it towards the boundary. Unfortunately for Bashar, it was a set up, and it worked. It was too early in his innings for such an expansive shot, and he holed out to long off. Lambu took the catch comfortably and threw the ball in the air in delight.

'Ha! I knew he wouldn't be able to resist,' Mahi celebrated. Indeed the whole team were ecstatic at the cheap dismissal of the Cricketeers' best batsman. Bashar left the wicket fuming, chastising himself with a whack of his pads with his bat.

The two players had crossed while the ball was in the air, and so Gauti was back on strike for the second ball. As an opener, he was more used to there being pace on the ball at the top of the innings. He had a look at his first ball from the spinner. Then caught in two minds against the next, he played a more attacking stroke than he might usually. A thin edge sliced the ball over the head of the slip fielder. A streaky four resulted, and Gauti breathed a sigh of relief.

If he was rattled by Bashar's dismissal and the near miss, his confidence returned with the third ball, which popped up invitingly to be hit. Frustratingly, for him, he smashed it straight to a fielder, who stopped a certain four. A bullet throw arrived in Mahi's gloves with a 'whoosh'. Tight fielding, saving ones and twos would help their cause no end, and no batsman liked to be becalmed. Gauti had let the occasion get to him, and the next ball did for him. A tentative prod, this time held by slip, meant that he'd trouble the scorers no further.

The BYC supporters jumped about with glee, and Ayesha and some of the girls did an impromptu twirly dance.

This brought Bhoo to the wicket for his first innings. He was there rather sooner than he'd expected, and the gaggle of spectators muttered excitedly. He looked around the pitch, counting the fieldsman. It was more of an act than anything else, trying to show the bowler who was in control.

'There are ten,' Mahi piped up from behind the stumps. 'Only just though. I have to keep counting them to make sure Doolally hasn't pinched another one.'

It was an unfair jibe. Bhoo had hardly chosen the circumstances in which he found himself. As the bowler started his run up, he did his best to banish any negatives thoughts from his mind. The bowler let the ball go, and his nerve held. He saw it clearly and played it into a gap past mid off for one. With a dot ball to end the second over, the Mumbai Cricketeers were 7 for 2.

The next over was hardly one for the cricket purist or spectator. A quick single to Bhoo at the start of it put Shaz on strike. He was finding it hard to gauge the pace of the wicket. He was normally a fluent player, but he flailed about, swinging at and missing four successive balls, each one bringing an 'OOOH' and an 'AAAH' from the keeper. Finally, he got some bat on one, and the ball trickled down to long leg. The batsmen jogged through for a single. With no run off the last ball, Shaz found himself on strike again for the start of the next over. Bashar could hardly contain himself on the boundary.

'What is he doing out there?' he demanded. 'Nine, just nine off the first three overs. It is useless!'

But worse was to come. Mahi made a bowling change, and Lambu picked up where the others had left off. His first ball was outside the off stump. Shaz did his best to drag it to leg but was unsuccessful. The next ball dipped in on him, pitched and straightened, whizzing over the middle stump. In fairness, it was as close to an unplayable delivery as one might get. When the following ball hit Mahi's gloves harmlessly, the Mumbai Cricketeers had only scored off half a dozen of the first twenty balls. For Shaz, some relief came from the next ball, although perhaps not in the way he'd have liked. Lambu bowled a slow bouncer, the ball sat up at chest height, and Shaz pulled it to the square leg fielder.

'OUT!' cried Woolly from the boundary before trying to high-five Uncle, who had no idea about high-fiving.

'Stop hitting me,' Uncle protested, ducking down.

Shaz walked off the ground slowly. As he arrived at the boundary's edge, he lobbed his bat and pieces of kit onto a pile of similar items in disgust.

Tiger had passed him on his way out and was already at the crease. He would have to play the ultimate captain's knock to save his team from here. Unfortunately, he'd been in a scrape with a cat the day before and had a black eye that was puffy and swollen. He'd found in practice that if he pulled a cap over it, he could see better through his good eye, but it was far from ideal.

The Cricketeers held their breath collectively as he faced his first ball. A swing, a click and a catch. Mahi threw the ball in the air with a loud appeal. The Cricketeers and their supporters let out their breath with a groan.

'He hit the ground,' Bumble explained. 'NOT OUT.'

'Well played the umpire!' Mr Doolally shouted. Which wasn't really in keeping with the spirit of cricket but was in character. He did, however, show that Bumble was going to call the game as he saw it and not take sides.

After this scare, things began to settle down, and Bhoo and Tiger started to rebuild the innings. Each of the batsmen found gaps in the field and a number of singles came and then successive boundaries. Finally, the Cricketeers' supporters had something to cheer.

Outside, at the back of the pavilion, Sunni had pedalled back to the gatekeeper's hut. There was a kafuffle going on between the gatekeeper and the DJ from the radio station.

'I tell you I have been invited. Look again at your list,' the DJ demanded.

The gatekeeper was adamant that everyone had been crossed off his list and that entry would not be permitted. Behind him on the wall of his cubicle was the same poster that Sunni had seen earlier.

'Look,' the DJ pointed to it. 'I'm on the radio "Jaldi Chalo, let's find this game a prize", that was me. You must have heard it.'

The gatekeeper scratched his chin; perhaps it did ring a bell.

'Look in the corner of the poster, there's even a photo of the old trophy. The little elephant trophy, goodness knows I've seen enough elephants in the last few days.' He pulled out a handkerchief and mopped his brow.

Sunni, who'd been sitting on the curb listening, suddenly realised the rickshaw was rolling. Before he could stop it, the whole thing dropped over the edge, landing on its front wheel before turning over. The wooden elephant spilled from the back of it and bounced, bumped and rolled to the DJ's feet.

Having recognised it from the poster, Sunni had decided to try and deliver it to the Centenary Game in the main stadium, but not quite in this way.

'What on earth is this?' said the DJ, bending down and examining the object.

'I don't believe it!' he exclaimed, holding it at arm's length so that he could compare it against the poster. 'This is it, man! The Bombay Duck Trophy. Look it says it right here.' He ran a finger along the carving. The DJ became very excited and grabbed the gatekeeper by the shoulders through the window of his little hut. 'You have to let me in, it's what the Centenary Game is all about, look at the poster, man!'

The DJ urged the gatekeeper to look at his list one more time. Sure enough, he'd made an error as the DJ and the producer of his show had been typed on the same line. When the producer had arrived, he'd crossed out both the names. The mystery solved, the DJ ran to the entrance of the pavilion and into the Cricket Club of India.

His job done, Sunni righted his rickshaw. A mudguard had bent out of shape and was jamming one of the wheels, and the handlebars had twisted. There was nothing he could do now; he'd have to sort it out later. So having abandoned his trusty ride, he scampered off to join the others.

Sunni arrived to find the Mumbai Cricketeers starting their fourteenth over. Tiger and Bhoo had steadied the ship with a partnership of 80. Now the mood of the two sets of supporters was more even. There was also a sense that everyone would prefer for the final to be a good game rather than a one-sided walkover.

After some overs of spin, which had produced several sixes, to delight the crowd, Mahi threw the ball to Ishy again. Anyone bowling a second spell might be forgiven for a wayward opener, and Ishy delivered his as a fast full toss on the leg stump. Bhoo helped it on its way, and as the pair completed their run, the fielder threw a looping catch into the wicketkeeper. It had not been Bhoo's finest or most destructive innings, but no one could challenge his commitment to the team that challenged his loyalty and went against his nature.

Tiger had coped with his injury admirably. He'd been a rock for the team. The solid defensive prod that he played to the next ball for a single was typical of the way he'd played. Bhoo, on the other hand, was starting to see the ball like the proverbial football.

Ishy, still struggling with his line, again bowled a wayward delivery, to which Bhoo played an ambitious reverse sweep. He made a good connection, if not out of the middle of the bat, and the pair ran two. Emboldened by this success, Bhoo looked to repeat the shot to the next ball. Ishy had deliberately bowled it slower, and the little mouse was through his shot too early. A bottom edge brought the death rattle, the sound of his stumps being broken.

'Don't look behind you, it's a horrible sight.' Mahi's send-off confirmed what he already knew. Bhoo trudged off to the applause of all the spectators, and Mr Doolally made a point of congratulating him personally.

'Well batted, boy. I didn't think you had it in you after all that fuss.' It was a bit of a backhanded compliment.

'May I go to my Uncle now, sir?' Bhoo asked.

'Yes, run along,' Doolally said, swatting him away like a fly.

Much to the relief of everybody on the BYC side, Bhoo was finally able to join them. Uncle hugged him and cried a bit, which everyone found touching.

'Excuse me,' Sunni called out, distracting everyone. 'May I take the field as twelfth man, Ump?'

Bumble waved him on, and Sunni got an opportunity to play on the Cricket Club of India's hallowed ground.

The over ended with the score on 94 for 4. Vishy was the new batsman at the crease, and with the partnership broken, there was work to be done to consolidate the position of the Cricketeers. Lambu came on again and succumbed to the same fate as Ishy, bowling some loose balls at the start of his new spell. A couple of singles were followed by a huge six, which drew gasps from the spectators. Two more singles meant ten had come off the over, a good return.

Ishy was back on song for the next, bowling fast and pinning the batsmen down and frustrating them. With five overs to go, the Cricketeers wanted to be scoring off every ball. Vishy's solid defence, the 'old school' approach, was not what they needed at this stage.

'This isn't a test match,' Bashar ranted from the boundary as he walked back and forth in front of the scoreboard.

So it was a relief in many ways when Vishy misjudged a rising ball and edged it to the keeper. The clear snick, prompted a huge cry of 'HOWZAT!' and Bumble's trigger finger did the rest. This bought Jaddu to the wicket. He strutted about, twiddled his bat and surveyed the field as if he were lord over all he surveyed. Ishy welcomed him with a bouncer to put him in his place. To give him his due, Jaddu dealt with it admirably, standing his ground whilst attempting a pull shot. It was too early in his innings for such an attacking shot, and although mistimed, it brought one run.

More spin followed, and the wily Jumbo spun his web. Jaddu, himself a spinner, was up to the test and dabbed the ball down for a single. Tiger decided to take him on, and the next ball produced a majestic six driven over mid off. Now the Cricketeers' spectators got involved. 'TIGER, TIGER!' they chanted. Jumbo bowled wide outside the off stump, Tiger tried to pull the ball all the way to leg and perished, instantly quietening the spectators. Seventy-three was an excellent score, however, and had saved the blushes of Doolally and the rest of his team. Tiger raised his bat in acknowledgement as everyone in the arena clapped.

The next batsman was Dev, the all-rounder, who took guard from Bumble and looked fierce. He wouldn't go down without a fight, and his cheeky paddle sweep for four off his first ball confirmed this. The over finished with the score on 121 for 6. Dev walked down the wicket and met Jaddu for a pow wow.

'Eighteen balls to go; we must bat all the way through,' he ordered. Jaddu made a fist and they punched gloves with a silent boing.

Yoovi came on to turn his arm over bowling off spin. He had all sorts of tricks up his sleeve when it came to slower balls, stuttered run-ups and where he delivered the ball from on the crease. The two elegant players were more than a match for him. They rotated the strike efficiently, working the ball around the ground. Add a couple of boundaries, and at the end of the over, they'd moved the score on to 133 for 6.

Both the batsman were starting to enjoy themselves. Bhajji came back on to bowl, and Dev despatched him for consecutive sixes. A massive, beautiful drive and in contrast, an agricultural hoick over cow corner. But Bhajji was always happy to buy a wicket, and he got his revenge off the next ball with a sharp return catch, easily pouched.

'I hope the tail wags,' Doolally, who'd wandered over to stand by Bashar, murmured. No sooner had he said this than Rookie had a huge swing and a miss and was bowled first ball. 'The commentator's curse,' Doolally spat and cracked his knuckles in fury. As Bhuvi walked out to the wicket, he called after him, 'Take no prisoners!'

'Hold up,' Bumble held up his hand to stop the bowler. He wandered out to the boundary and scolded Doolally for threatening behaviour. 'I might start issuing yellow cards to some spectators, so watch it.'

Back on the field, Bhajji's hat-trick ball was an anti-climax, the ball sticking in his paw and going for a wide. This was followed by a four pushed over the boundary as the fielder slipped and then a nicely timed cut shot. They were precious runs indeed. The scoreboard read 154 for 8 with an over to go.

A final over of pace followed. No tail-ender really likes fast bowling, but Bhuvi was no tail-ender, and he struck the first ball smartly. However, a magnificent stop restricted him to one. Another single to rotate the strike and then Bhuvi was felled attempting to go for a big one. With Zak left, not much was expected, and indeed not much was produced. They managed a single and then a run out off the last ball trying to turn one into two. The game had swung both ways, but 158 all out was a lot more runs than it looked as though the Cricketeers would get at one stage. It was a fighting score on a pitch that might test the BYC.

'That was an excellent effort, guys,' Woolly cried, rallying his players. 'It was particularly good to snaffle you-know-who at the top of the order.'

Bhoo hung back from the group to talk to Uncle.

'How do you think the rest of the team will welcome me, Uncle?'

'I have a feeling they'll be pretty pleased to see you,' Uncle replied with a smile.

'How can you be so sure?' Bhoo asked.

'Because when you bat for us, I've got AJ's bat for you.'

Bhoo

## Chapter Sixteen

A snooty doorman had helped the DJ negotiate his way through the club and out onto the packed terrace overlooking the playing area. Here there was a mass of specially invited guests milling around. He helped himself to a handful of spicy mix from a bowl and fed it to himself as he surveyed the scene. Who'd be the best person, he wondered, to approach in this melee about his find.

On the playing area stretched out in front of them, the players trudged from the field, a good-natured game having reached its midpoint. The England team had batted first and compiled an impressive total off their forty overs. Their well-practiced and tested athletes no match for the Indian Invitational XI. Their opposition had been picked more on a 'who's who' of Indian cricket than a cream of the current crop basis. A number of the 'past greats' had clearly not spent a lot, if any, time in the gym before the match. Relying on their gift for the game and in some cases their roly-poly physique to see them through.

On the terrace, General Baig entertained a gaggle of ladies in brightly coloured saris with tales of derring-do. A well-known ex-captain of the Indian team was doing a similar job to a collection of businessman, who'd turned into wide-eyed schoolboys in the presence of their hero. A lot of fuss was being made of Mr Ram Verma, the DJ read his name badge, of Holistic Holi Powders Ltd. by another crowd of guests.

The DJ continued to weave his way through the gathering. Nearby, the easy laugh of a club member caught his attention. Clearly he was revelling in the opportunity to show off his club. Behind him, seated on his own in a corner, was an old gentleman swathed in a shawl.

'Is this seat taken?' the DJ asked of the old boy.

'No, sit... sit, keep me company,' Colonel Kulkarni replied.

'Are you enjoying the game?'

'Yes indeed. What a spectacle it is with the stadium full.'

'Fantastic that the England team were able to fit the game into their itinerary,' the DJ said, struggling to make conversation.

'I met them you know? Well, him... the England captain, in London before they left for the subcontinent,' Kulkarni announced proudly.

The colonel proceeded to tell the DJ the story of his trip to London and his association with the Bombay Brothers. As the old colonel trotted out his tale about the wartime cricket and the little trophy associated with it, the DJ listened intently.

'In that case, you may be interested to see this.' The DJ rummaged in his pocket and pressed the little wooden elephant into the old man's hands.

Colonel Kulkarni held the object up and looked down his nose through his glasses at it. He turned it over carefully in his aged and bony fingers. Not only did it fit the description of the historic object, but there, carved on its base, was the unmistakable inscription.

'But what is this?' he said in disbelief.

'I think it is just what this game's been looking for,' said the DJ, enjoying the fact that his idea to find the game a fitting prize had turned full circle. Here he was presenting *the* trophy to the very person who was best qualified to receive it.

'We must tell them!' The old man became as animated as his frail body would allow. 'Help me up, young man.' But as he got to his feet, an announcement came over the ground's public address system. The England side was taking the field for the Indian Invitation XI's innings. This caused the guests on the terrace to surge forward, and the old man was lost in the sea of people.

## Chapter Seventeen

As the Indian Invitational XI's openers strode out to face the England attack, so too did the Gabbar and Chiku for the Bombay Yacht Club. It was decided that Bunni, who was more used to opening, was too slow at scoring and should bat down the order. It was a hard call, and Bunni sat away from the others for a while, sunglasses on and cap firmly pulled down.

Tiger had called his team around him for a pre-innings huddle.

'First, thanks to Beaky, who is from England and is going to field for us.' The team acknowledged Beaky, who'd volunteered. 'Let's back up our bowlers, stay tight on the singles, no silly overthrows and no blaming each other either.' He cast a rueful look at Bashar, who chose to ignore it. With that, the team broke away and jogged off onto the pitch.

'159 to get—that's eight an over,' Woolly informed the openers. 'No need, to go crazy from ball one, have a look at it, punish the loose ball and try not to throw your wicket away.' It was all very well for him to say, but there was a lot that was unknown for the batsmen, and just what exactly the Cricketeers' 'pressure cooker' had in store for them.

Bumble was back at his post, gave the left-hander, Gabbar, a guard of leg stump and bellowed 'PLAY!' Shortly followed by 'WIDE!' as Zak, the opening bowler, strayed down the leg side with his first delivery. The BYC were off the mark.

Zak's left-arm over-the-wicket bowling was trickier for a right-handed batsman, and Gabbar's left-handedness cancelled this out. His first over continued to be wayward, and Gabbar was able to clip a four off the second ball, which strayed onto his pads. A succession of misdirected balls of varying length, bounce and velocity followed, bringing more runs. The over culminated in a crazy bouncer that stranded the wicketkeeper, clearing him completely and going for four wides.

Somewhat shell-shocked, with 11 on the board after just one over, Tiger threw the ball to Bhuvi. He was quite harmless in appearance with bright eyes and neatly combed fur, but he had venomous pace. Chiku was now on strike. He strode down the pitch and deftly flicked a microscopic obstruction from the wicket. Back in his crease, he fiddled with his gloves and then acknowledged Bumble with a brief tip of his helmet. He rested his bat on his shoulder and studied the fielders' positions. It was all theatre, a display that said 'I am in charge here, you need to fear me.' But if that was the case, Bhuvi wasn't paying attention.

The first ball of the over was very quick and spat up at Chiku, who flung one hand off the bat. The ball had jarred his thumb against the handle, and he shook it painfully. Surely this was an aberration and normal service would soon be resumed. He'd been in a rich vein of form, almost scoring at will in earlier games. So when he survived only three balls, the third cannoning into the stumps off the inside edge of his bat, the BYC spectators gasped.

In his head, Woolly mentally tore up his game plan. He tried not to show his concern as he greeted his star player with a consoling arm around the shoulder. Chiku punched the back of his bat as if it was to blame.

Chiku's dismissal brought Bhoo back to the wicket. As he walked out, Bashar brushed past him.

'You are not as bad as people say—you are much, much worse,' he sneered. It was the sort of banter that the Australians normally save for the English.

Bhoo did his best to ignore it and gave his bat a twiddle. Perhaps his nerves had got the better of him, but he was convinced he felt it twitch in his paws.

'Right arm over, three to come!' Bumble boomed.

Bhoo glanced furtively round the field and settled over his bat. Bhuvi bowled and Bhoo, carrying on from where he left off in his previous innings, played a controlled stoke into the covers. Vishy obliged with a horrible misfield, which prompted a tirade from Bashar, and Bhoo jogged through for a single to get off the mark.

Having crossed, Gabbar twitched about the crease. He'd been unnerved by Bhuvi's opening salvo, which had troubled Chiku. He had reason to be and there was more to come. The next ball, a well-directed short ball, hit him on the helmet, and he had to take a moment to compose himself.

'All right, fella?' Bumble called down the pitch.

Gabbar acknowledged him and play resumed. Whether it was bravado on his part or just a lucky connection, but he slap-slogged the next ball, just clearing mid wicket, and the ball ran away for four. The little crowd clapped their appreciation, and Woolly blew a wolf-whistle.

The batsmen met in the middle of the pitch.

'You're sure you're okay?' Bhoo asked his partner.

'Sure, he just rattled my eyeballs a bit.' Gabbar pulled a face, wobbled his head and rolled his eyes until they were crossed.

Despite his first effort with the ball, Zak was given a second over. However, Bhoo had the measure of him, and he carefully defended the first couple of balls. If he needed a 'sighter', then those were it. Taking a stride down the wicket, Bhoo made a fantastic connection with the next ball, sending it back over Bumble's head for six.

'What a shot!' the wicketkeeper cried out from behind him.

'Is it just me or did that ball just flash as it hit 'is bat?' Bumble rubbed his eyes. He wasn't the only one taken aback by it as Bhoo looked at the face of his blade in disbelief.

As the spectators and fielders contemplated the booming six that had just taken place, Bhoo played a late cut with finesse that ran between the slips for a single. The now skittish Gabbar survived the over and scrambled a leg bye off the last ball.

'That is quite a bat,' Gabbar observed during their mid-wicket chat.

'Yes, it is a VVS bat from Mr AJ.'

'Ahh, that explains a lot,' said Gabbar with a punch of his glove.

Gabbar could have done with an AJ bat too, as his just didn't seem wide enough. He was well beaten by Bhuvi's first delivery of the next over, and the second, a fast in-swinging yorker, clean bowled him.

On the edge of the ground, Woolly hastily re-jigged the batting order, holding back Bunni again. Dervall, who had a reputation for being solid in defence, strode out instead. With Bhuvi on such a hot streak, he'd have to do a good impression of a wall to keep him out.

There was a slight improvement inasmuch as Dervall managed to lay a bat on Bhuvi's next ball. The downside was that it went straight to slip—two wickets in two balls. Woolly threw his hat down in frustration.

'Come on, guys,' he moaned, cramming the bobble hat back on his head. The next batsman and his rumbustious style provided some hope, and he sent him off with a cry of 'Go get 'em Yoovi!'

Yoovi's mind for the time being was concentrated on not being the victim of a hat-trick. Tiger crowded his fielders around the new batsman and a hush settled over the spectators as Bhuvi ran in to bowl. Down came the ball, everyone held their breath, and Yoovi stopped it dead with a formidable forward defence. The little bit of drama over, the fielders returned to their normal positions and the over finished as a maiden. It had been an excellent over that had rocked the BYC and saw the bowler return figures of 3 for 5.

Some respite came for the batsmen with the introduction of spin. Jaddu handed his cap to Bumble and marked out his run up. Bhoo had now relaxed and appeared to be brimming with confidence. He watched the first ball carefully and punched the ball with the spin off the back foot. Yoovi always liked to see the scoreboard ticking over and was keen to get off the mark. He played an ugly swish at his first ball from Jaddu, and the ball dropped a little way in front of him.

'Yes!' he called. Jaddu sprinted to where the ball had landed.

'Wait!' Yoovi cried. Then 'No!' this made Jaddu miss the ball altogether, to which Yoovi yelled 'Yes!' again.

Bhoo was shimmying in and out of his crease like a Bollywood dancer and reacting to his partner's unconventional call, he scrambled home to complete the run.

'Sorry!' Yoovi apologised. As if to show him how it should be done, Bhoo prodded the next ball into a space and called 'one' firmly.

This did little to settle Yoovi, and by the fourth ball of the over, he too was back in the 'hutch' pulling the ball to mid-wicket having caught the ball on the toe end of the bat. It was a soft dismissal soon to be followed in the next over by another as Bhajji drove the ball into to mid on's paws. The incoming batsmen were all looking for a big shot to release the pressure while only adding to it.

Now Tiger was happy to give Bhoo a single. He was keen to get him off strike so that they could concentrate their efforts on the new batsman. Mahi had come in to settle the ship, and if ever there was a mouse for a crisis, he was it. With five wickets down, from now on, neither mouse took any risks. Singles came and the odd four, and by the start of the ninth over, the BYC needed 112 off 72 balls.

Bashar decided that he should turn his arm over, as bowling seemed so easy. Tiger caved in to his pressure, and Bhoo and Mahi took advantage of it. First, an all-run three to Bhoo before Mahi took him to task. Two fours came as Mahi used his feet to the inexperienced bowler. Now rattled, Bashar bowled a wide and then a long hop, which Mahi bashed for six. Eighteen off the over gave the BYC fans something to cheer, and even Woolly stopped moaning for an instant.

Tiger decided it was time to seek the help of his dependable lieutenant, and Shaz came on to bowl. This staunched the flow of runs, and each of the batsmen was restricted to successive singles. Mahi, not one to be tied down for long, swung across the line of what he thought was an easy slower ball, but Shaz's arm ball trapped him dead in front of the stumps.

'HOWZAT!' shouted Shaz.

'OUT!' replied Bumble.

'We're not having LBW... we agreed,' Mahi complained.

'I've given him out I'm afraid, and there are no reviews in mouse cricket.'

The LBW rule had been discussed before Bumble took over the umpiring. Now that this had worked in their favour, the Cricketeers were happy to accept Bumble's decision. It was a body blow to the BYC, and with the slow scoring Bunni now at the wicket, things were not looking good.

They were now halfway through their overs, and the score stood at 70-6. With Bhoo at the wicket, the BYC still had a chance, but it was a slim one. Jaddu had the ball in his paw and strutted about looking important. He tinkered with the field, making minor adjustments here and there.

At the end of the over, Bunni didn't make eye contact with Bhoo, and as a result, they stayed at their respective ends. Despite the fact that there had been no mid-wicket conference, Bhoo gave the impassive Bunni a friendly wave. Again there was no response from his partner. Everyone had their own method he decided, and with that, he shrugged and settled over his bat. A dot ball and a single brought Bunni to the striker's end. The demotion down the order seemed to have the desired effect on

Bunni's strike rate, as a full toss, declared a 'NO BALL' by Bumble, was struck for two.

'FREE HIT!' Bumble declared, with which Bashar took issue. 'For overstepping the line, you have a free hit, and that's an end to it.'

The ball was bowled again. It was a 'gimmie', right in the slot, asking to be hit, and Bunni obliged, depositing the ball over the boundary for six. Woolly was amazed by the seismic change in the batter's performance. The BYC followers were enthusiastic in their support and cheered and waved.

'Way to go, Bunni!' shouted Ayesha.

Slowly the unlikely pair built a partnership, rotating the strike and running sharp singles. Turning ones into twos and hitting the loose ball to the boundary. The score crept towards the hundred mark. With three off the thirteenth and four of the fourteenth overs, the viewing for the BYC spectators was painful. It was edge-of-the-seat stuff, and there was a fair amount of nervous claw nibbling. The Cricketeers fast bowlers still had overs in hand and would make life difficult bowling at the death. If Bhoo and Bunni were going to do it, now was the time to go for it.

The fifteenth over started with a dot ball and then a single, bringing Bhoo to the striker's end. He looked about him, trying to pinpoint any gaps. With many of the fielder's on the edge of the field, it was going to be difficult to score the necessary boundaries. Bhoo held his bat like a 'lightsabre' and called on it to help him now.

'If ever there was a time for a Very Very Special bat, this is it,' he whispered to it.

The next ball came in fast and kept low. The bat twitched in Bhoo's paws and the ball met its sweet spot. Bumble leapt in the air as the ball travelled over the opposite set of stumps and missed him by a fraction. Two fielders in the deep sprinted to field it, but the ball shot between them, leaving them in an awkward embrace. Furious to concede a four, the bowler strode back to his mark and raced in again. A bouncer outside off stump, and Bhoo flailed the bat. A poor connection, a mishit in fact, but the ball took off like a rocket and cleared the boundary.

'SIX!' cried Beaky, forgetting he was on the wrong side.

Bashar snarled in his direction.

Then a chance, a flat hit that reached the fielder at an awkward height. Dive and catch or flounder and stop it. The fielder opted for the second, saving a run and maybe more. With two run off the last ball of the over, it had been a profitable one, and Bashar berated the besieged Tiger.

'Take the pace off the ball, bowl spin!' he ordered.

So spin it was, and Bhoo easily lifted the first ball over square leg and the boundary with a perfectly timed sweep shot. A nicely worked single followed, and it felt to everyone in the arena as if the momentum of the game had edged to the Bombay Yacht Club. The mice putting up the score rummaged about for the correct numbers and adjusted the total to 117 for 6. The Mumbai Cricketeers had been on 107 for 4 at the same stage. As if to compound matters, Bunni joined the party, helping a full toss over the wicketkeeper's head, registering the second six of the over. The BYC fans went mad, jumping up and down hugging each other. The poor bowler had succumbed to the increasing pressure with a terrible, wayward over.

The seventeenth over started. The run chase was definitely on, and Bhoo's score had moved into the sixties. Things were clearly pretty tense in the Cricketeers' camp. A cheeky single off the first ball only added to it. Dev, the bowler, tried to kick the ball onto the stumps but only succeeded in kicking it past the keeper. Bashar ranted and Tiger appealed for calm. But the atmosphere was tense and tempers were starting to fray. The Cricketeers might be a rag-tag assortment of players, but they all wanted to win. So when Bhoo hit the next ball a country mile for six, the Cricketeers went into meltdown.

'Whose brainwave was it to give the ball to Dev?' Bashar complained.

'Dev is a great 'death bowler', Tiger defended his decision.

'That was a great big hit; we can all agree on that,' Rookie chipped in.

'I'll show you, give me that ball,' Dev snapped.

The next ball was a stunning—with a capital 'S'—comeback. Bowled out of the back of his hand, a slower ball that saw the batsman complete his shot before it was past him. There had been no discernible change in the bowler's action, which was a neat trick.

With both batsmen favouring the leg side, Tiger packed it with fielders. The response from Bhoo was predictable, if difficult to execute, and a reverse sweep sent the ball to the fence for four. On top of that, a single to end the over kept him on strike. Bhoo's performance for his rightful team had been marvellous, and the Cricketeers only hope, it seemed, was to knock him over.

The eighteenth over started with the BYC on 138 for 6. They needed twenty-one off the last eighteen balls, a finely balanced equation for either side. One that was less well balanced after

Bhoo managed to get away with another cheeky little dab reverse sweep for four, which was met with cries from various fielders of 'I told you we needed a third man.' Then a moment for the other team. Dev bowled an uncharacteristic loopy, slower ball that Bhoo missed. Such was his momentum that he swung himself round in a full circle and the ball struck him on the leg.

'HOWZAT!' shouted the whole Cricketeers team in unison.

'Not out,' Bumble answered them calmly.

'BOOOOOOOOO!' the spectators on one side of the arena cried as one.

As the boos subsided, Dev, who'd marched back to his mark chuntering to himself, conspired to bowl a leg-side wide. It was a tough call, but by the letter of the law, Bumble was spot on. The bowler was livid and his teammates couldn't believe he'd done it. Poor Tiger held his head in his paws. If ever there was a panic button in a team's kit bag, the Cricketeers appeared to have one and to have pushed it!

Dev, still erring down the leg side, enabled Bhoo to whip the ball down to long leg for a single. The BYC were cruising now at a run a ball, having been 29 for 5. It was unlike Dev to be so wayward, but having started the over badly things, were about to get worse. A short-pitched bouncer, fuelled by frustration, sat up waiting to be hit, and Bunni obliged. Four more.

'BUNNI! BUNNI!' the BYC supporters chanted. It was out of character for the normally shy player to be centre stage. Perhaps Bunni thrived on pressure, but most batsman will agree that in their best innings, they've had a slice of luck. Bunni's luck duly arrived in the form of an inside edge that missed the leg stump by the thinnest coat of varnish.

Rookie, behind the stumps, was sold a dummy and the ball sped to the fence for a streaky four. He stood with his paws on his hips, wondering how their winning position of just fifteen overs before had evaporated.

'Unlucky, Dev!' he called out, trying to reinvigorate his teammate. But it was to no avail as Bunni hit the next ball through the covers to complete a hat-trick of boundaries. The scoreboard was adjusted, and the simple arithmetic of the situation was that the Bombay Yacht Club needed just three off twelve balls. It had been an unbelievable run chase. Bhoo had been truly brilliant, and AJ's bat, well, who knew what AJ did to his bats. Also, Bunni's match-winning support had turned the game on its head.

As the nineteenth over began, the BYC supporters and players lined up along the edge of the boundary. Bhuvi was a skilled 'death' bowler, but only the most extreme intervention by Mr Doolally would swing the game to the Cricketeers. The batsmen met in the centre of the wicket.

'No risks, just play it cool,' Bhoo advised.

Bunni stared back impassively.

A single off the first ball rotated the strike and brought Bunni down to face the next ball. Bhuvi, searching for a slow yorker, bowled a full toss, and Bunni played the ball to mid off for one. Bhoo had sprinted the first run and, noticing the tiniest miss-field, called for a second. The fielder hurled the ball into the bowler's end, Bhoo ran his bat in, and Bumble leapt in the air. The ball passed the stumps without disturbing the bails and the run was completed.

'HOLY GUACAMOLLY!' shouted Woolly, throwing his hat in the air.

This sparked a pitch invasion by the Bombay Yacht Club. Bhoo ran about with his bat raised while Bunni made a low-key, more intense personal celebration, clenching a fist and shaking it.

As everyone ran around jumping up and down and cheering, Ayesha came running out of the melee and leapt at Bunni. Not expecting it, the resulting collision knocked Bunni's helmet and sunglasses off.

'Eeeee!' Bunni cried as the reason for all the mystery was revealed. Everyone had assumed that Bunni was a 'he' when in actual fact *she* was not!

'Well I never,' Woolly stuttered, cramming his hat on the back of his head in disbelief.

'How brilliant, go girl!' cried Ayesha.

'YAAAY,' cried the other girls who'd swarmed around her.

The relief of having her secret out in the open at last freed Bunni to join in the celebrations properly.

Doolally sidled up to Bumble as he left the pitch. 'I say, does that mean the match is void, Umpire?'

'NO!' Bumble replied definitely. 'If anything, it makes the result even better. Now run along and hand that cup over to the winning captain.'

'My boy,' Uncle gushed as he hobbled up to his protégé. 'What a star you are. Everyone back home at Dharavi will be so proud. I can't wait to tell everyone. Particularly AJ; I'm sure there are going to be lots of little batsman wanting a Bhoo bat. You're a hero.'

As the celebrations subsided, everyone gathered around the scoreboard, where Mr Doolally had stationed himself to grudgingly relinquish his team's hold on the trophy.

Mr Googly had made it for the presentation having missed most of the match. He'd struggled to make it up the ducting having urged the others to go on ahead.

'Aha, Doolally, at last we've managed to prise your claws off the cup.'

'If you're happy to cheat and manipulate the rules, then it would seem so.' Doolally was not particularly generous with his compliments in defeat.

'Eee, excuse me,' Bumble said, hovering at his side. 'I'd just present the cup if I were you unless you'd like to explain your methods of team selection.' Bumble pretended to sneeze whilst saying the word 'kidnap' and Doolally got the message.

'If you'd all like to gather round,' Doolally addressed all the mice. Eventually the excited hubbub died down and he continued.

'I would just like to say that we've all enjoyed an excellent game of cricket here in this fantastic setting. Although some of the players didn't perform quite as expected...'

'If you can't say anything nice, don't say anything at all!' Uncle jeered unexpectedly.

'Ah, yes, ahem...' Doolally collected himself after the interruption. 'In that case, without further ado, if the captain of the Bombay Yacht Club team would like to step up.'

Mahi edged his way through the crowd and collected the trophy from Mr Doolally. As he held it up aloft, a huge roar from the crowd in the main part of the stadium outside erupted. This prompted a spontaneous movement for the celebrations to move outside.

As soon as the players of the Mumbai Cricketeers, none of whom had enjoyed Mr Doolally's regime, picked up on this, they urged the visitors to follow them.

'Come on, everybody, this way!' cried Jaddu, skipping across the playing area. He led them to a hole that opened onto another length of spiral ducting. Through this, they were able to get to the bottom of the tower. The trip down was considerably quicker and easier than the trip up, and even Mr Googly made it down. In no time, the entire visiting mouse population found themselves in a narrow tunnel with a view of the pitch. The atmosphere from the main event poured down it and enveloped them.

## Chapter Eighteen

On the main ground, the game had been a slight mismatch. The Indian selectors had been keen to keep their international players under wraps until the international series started. A good-humoured crowd had been happy to cheer their favourites of the recent past. However, the well-practised England outfit had been just too strong for the Invitational XI and wickets had tumbled regularly. A glittering cameo by one of Mumbai's favourite sons had been the highlight of the innings. It was the roar of his hitting a six that had coincided with Mahi's lifting of the area trophy. But following his dismissal, hope of a win for the hosts had waned. The last tail-enders had fallen in quick succession, and the home side's innings had come to a close well short of the total set for them by the visitors.

As one side met the other on the outfield for a series of handshakes, preparations were being made for the presentation ceremony. A hoarding proclaimed that Holistic Holi Powders Ltd. were 'Proud to sponsor the Bombay Brothers Centenary Match.'

When everything was in position, the presentation party made their way out to the hoarding, and the two teams took their places either side of it. Mr Ram Verma had been making an urgent call and missed the procession, joining the group looking slightly flustered. The call he'd been making was to ensure that the 'local colour' he'd mentioned at the hotel press conference was in place. Behind the scenes, in a corridor that normally gave access to the heavy machines used to tend the ground, waiting calmly, despite the crowd noise, was an elaborately decorated and painted elephant and his mahout.

The mice ventured out of their hiding place and scurried out to take up a vantage point behind the advertising boards round the ground.

'Wow, this is awesome,' Compo exclaimed to Sunni as they looked out onto the packed stadium.

'Yes, there is no place quite like it.'

Bumble and Beaky were both squashed together trying to look through the same gap.

'Will you give over?' Bumble grumbled.

Their bickering was interrupted by an electronic buzz as General Baig adjusted the microphone, which didn't need adjusting, in front of him.

'What a feast of cricket we've enjoyed,' he began. The crowd responded with suitable fervour. 'Cricketing greats...' which was greeted with another roar, '...and friends from overseas,' which received polite applause. An enormously long list of 'thank yous' followed.

As the general addressed the stadium, two lines of children from local schools, each of them holding a small packet, were ushered onto the ground. They took up their stations in front of the two teams of players.

'Now, it is my great pleasure to invite Mr Singh and Mr Kumar to make commemorative presentations to the team captains,' the general boomed over the public address system. 'Then Colonel Kulkarni will present the Holistic Holi Powders Ltd...' the general adjusted his tie uncomfortably as he negotiated the mouthful, '...trophy to the winning captain.'

Gogi and Moti dutifully took their places and took it in turns to hand over engraved salvers to each of the team captains. More handshakes and photos followed, and then Colonel Kulkarni took centre stage. A smartly dressed bearer from the club hovered, holding the trophy in white-gloved hands. The old man grasped the microphone and bent it sharply down towards himself. The local sound engineer, who was monitoring the proceedings, shuddered and the colonel began to speak.

'The good general has explained to you all why we three are here.' He stretched out his arms as if to encompass Gogi and Moti. 'A direct link to those brave soldiers of the past, who, miles from home, were united by this great game of ours. If the captain of the England team would like to join me, I'd like to present *the Bombay Duck Trophy.*'

The bearer took a step forward with the trophy, and the England captain stepped up to receive it.

Colonel Kulkarni then produced the little wooden elephant from his pocket and held it up in the air. The crowd in the stadium roared their approval and the children threw their packages at the cricketers, covering them in multi-coloured Holistic Holi paints. The mahout took his cue and led out his elephant. The crowd roared its approval again.

Bumble and Beaky couldn't contain themselves and rushed out to join in the fun. Soon one of them was red and the other green.

Bumble was just going to wave to the others to join them when he spotted a man running towards them. It was Terry Packer, the team kit man.

'Oh heck, we've been rumbled,' he blubbered, grabbing Beaky by the arm. But the man wasn't interested in them. He stopped inches away and spoke over them.

'Quick it's happening!' Terry exclaimed.

The two mice raised their heads to see to whom this was directed. Rising, like a colossus above them, was one of the England fast bowlers splashed with splodges of different coloured paint.

'What? The baby? Now?' he gasped.

'Yes, we've got you booked on a flight home tonight. Someone's getting your kit together, and there'll be a car out front in fifteen minutes. You pick up your ticket at the airline desk.'

The young bowler had warned the team management that, as his wife was expecting their first child, he might have to pop home. The 'higher-ups' had assured him that they'd whisk him back to the UK if needs be, and indeed it appeared they were as good as their word.

'Did you hear that, Bumble?' Beaky cried, shaking his friend.

'I did indeed, old son. It sounds like we may be able to get a ride home. Quick, let's get Compo.'

Without a second glance, Bumble ran back to where the other mice were hiding. Just at this moment, the mahout led his elephant in front of the two teams. It may be a myth that elephants are scared of mice, but this elephant clearly believed it. With a loud trumpet, she reared away from the two rodents.

Ignoring the commands of her mahout, she then trotted off around the stadium. As every spare groundsman and security guard was pressed into catching up with her, the mice scrambled back to their friends.

'Compo, listen!' Beaky seized his friend by the shoulders and earnestly explained their exit strategy.

'But what about all our friends?'

'We've just got enough time to say goodbye to them, then we need to get outta here.'

The three friends grabbed Sunni and explained the opportunity that had suddenly presented itself.

'Of course, you must go,' Sunni agreed, and he rounded up the others to say farewell.

'But, Bumble, you could be such a good dancer,' moaned Ayesha.

'Do you really think so?' Bumble said, smoothing his whiskers with a licked paw.

'Of course, she doesn't. She's being polite,' Beaky scolded.

'Thank you so much for everything,' the mice repeated as they went around the group exchanging high-fives and hugs.

'Congratulations, Bhoo. You were amazing,' Compo complimented the tiny batsman, who looked at his toes and blushed. 'Maybe we'll see you at Lord's one day!'

'Nice to meet you, boys,' Woolly called out after them. 'Remember, practice, practice, practice,' he said, miming a forward defensive shot.

'How are you all going to get home, now that you've put you know who's nose out of joint?' Compo asked Sunni.

'Don't think you're the only ones grand enough to travel with the England cricket team!' Sunni replied with a grin. 'We'll all be heading back to the hotel with the team later. But come on now, we'd better get a move on.'

At that moment, the elephant galumphed by, distracting everyone. With a final wave, the three English mice took their leave of their friends and followed Sunni. He clearly knew his way around and led them straight into the deserted passage that ran through the middle of the building.

Terry had obligingly left the bowler's kit bag by the entrance doors.

'Give us a bunk up,' Bumble said over his shoulder, and the three other mice put their shoulders into lifting him. Bumble scrabbled up and pulled the zip open just enough give them access. The mice took it in turns to pull each other up, slipping through the opening. Beaky pulled Compo up, waved to Sunni, and then dropped out of sight.

'Come with us? Compo said to Sunni. 'You never know, you might get a ride back with the Indian team one day.'

'Thanks for the offer, but I think I'll stay just where I am.' He took off his cap with a flourish as a farewell salute.

Compo acknowledged it with a wave and disappeared from view.

'Achha chalte hain... goodbye,' Sunni called after them.

The England bowler appeared from the bowels of the building after a rapid shower. As he looped his hand through the bag handles, the club doors opened and a driver looked in.

'Airport, boss?' he enquired.

Compo

## Chapter Nineteen

It was raining at Heathrow. The young man looked out of the window of the taxi heading down the M4 motorway into London. The landscape was so familiar but so bland in comparison to the one he'd left behind. His focus was on his wife and the imminent arrival of a baby fast bowler, or bowlerette. He called his parents and got their exact coordinates, the 8th floor of St Thomas' Hospital, just opposite the Houses of Parliament. It was an auspicious location for the arrival of one's first child.

The driver dropped him by a sign pointing the way to the Florence Nightingale Museum outside the hospital. He then continued his journey over Westminster Bridge, through Parliament Square, round St James's Park, down The Mall, past Buckingham Palace, along Park Lane and on to Lord's Cricket Ground.

Sid Pickett was in residence at the Grace Gates.

'How may I help you, young man?' he asked of the taxi driver.

'I've got a bag that needs to go to...' he consulted his notes, '...the Cricket Office.'

'No problem at all. You can leave it with me.'

As the taxi executed a U-turn and sped off, Sid called the Facilities Department.

'When you've got a mo', I need a bag collected from Grace Gates and taken to the Cricket Office.'

A short time later, a battery-operated cart whirred by, collected the bag and then dropped it off at the appointed place. All this time, the mice sat tight, waiting for the bag to finish its stop-start journey. Eventually, they stopped with a jolt. A grunt was heard as they were heaved off the cart, an exchange of voices, a shuffling sound and the bang of a door.

'Where do you think we are?' Beaky whispered.

'Home, I reckon,' Bumble purred.

'Shhhh!' Compo warned.

Sitting sandwiched in the layers of kit on the floor of the office, they now had an agonising wait. They listened to the office banter. To the orders for coffee, telephone conversations and the comings and goings of a great many people. The Cricket Office, it seemed, was the centre of the Lord's universe—not really surprising for the home of cricket. Eventually, however, the working day came to an end, and the office closed its door for the day.

Keen not to jump the gun, the mice continued to wait in the darkness. After a suitable period of silence, the three friends emerged from their hiding place. They found themselves surrounded by boxes and piled-up stuff. Whether its location right next to the recently demolished Warner Stand was to blame for this fact, or perhaps that, from the small room, 500 matches at home and abroad every year are organised. Whatever their reason for being there, the mice used the objects as stepping-stones to skip across the room. From a desktop, they slipped into the fabric of the building through a hole under an overloaded shelf.

'We'll make our way to the Sleeping Room, and from there, we'll be able to see if anyone is around,' Compo stated, taking control.

They'd have to make their way up into the old pavilion before descending to their underground home. Through the age-old, blackened Victorian dust they wormed their way, breaking cover briefly to squeeze through a crack that brought them into the Old Library. Then back behind the wall's plaster and up using, as a ladder, the lath strips through which the ancient plaster bulged. They were on their way to the Writing Room at one end of the pavilion. The mice referred to it as the Sleeping Room because it seemed to have that effect on the members of the club. They passed behind the fireplace and paused to look through a hole in the wall that married up with a hole in the eye of the 'Captain of the Eleven'. For a brief moment, life flickered behind the unblinking eye of the boy in the Victorian painting. A red and yellow sticker on the wall beside it declared 'To be moved for conservation.' Soon, this spy-hole would be sealed, but they'd find another soon enough. In the room, a waiter was laying up the tables for the Author's Cricket Club annual dinner later that evening.

'Henry,' his supervisor called, 'could you come here a moment?'

The young man looked over his shoulder. 'The Captain of the Eleven' returned to being frozen in time and the mice found themselves alone.

'Quick, now that the coast is clear, let's get out of here,' Compo hissed.

The mice slithered down the dusty lining of the wall and out into a corridor through a tight squeeze. McCrackers, one of the club's quirkier members, known for his collection of colourful blazers, was reading the noticeboard. Now very much on the home straight, the mice tiptoed past him. Just as they were about to limbo under the double doors to the Long Room, he exploded.

'NOT...'

The mice froze.

'...tinghamshire are playing Middlesex in the County Championship on my birthday. Splendid, I'll make a day of it!' he exclaimed.

The mice guiltily continued on their way. Ahead of them stretched the great expanse of the Long Room, and a familiar smell wafted up to meet them.

'Do you smell that?' squeaked Beaky.

'I'd recognise that floor polish anywhere,' Bumble answered.

'Smells like home,' Compo added dreamily.

Together, the three globetrotting mice started to run. They ran as if their lives depended on it, all of them eager to be reunited with their friends. At the end of the room, they slid beneath one of the cabinets and dropped below floor level.

Compo ran ahead, following the well-worn route down to the mouse colony. As the others reached him, they found him sitting despondently in front of the entrance.

'Oh no,' Beaky said simply.

In front of them, a freshly cut piece of pine board had been fixed over the entry point. Four shiny cross-headed screws marked the four corners.

'What now?' Bumble asked.

'They must still be here, they can't have...' he swallowed hard.

'Oh 'eck...' Bumble staggered backwards as the realisation of what Compo was saying hit him. As he did so a loud 'SNAP' sounded behind him.

'YEEOUCH!' cried Bumble. 'THEY'VE GOT ME!'

Behind him a single mousetrap had been fired, trapping his tail.

'I'm a goner, guys, save yourselves... goodbye, cruel world!' Bumble wailed melodramatically.

'TOO LATE!' Beaky shrieked as a blinding light cut through the darkness. The three mice dropped their heads and awaited their fate. The beam swept past, over and above them.

'Will you hold that thing steady,' Beefy scolded.

'I'm doing my best,' Fred complained.

'Beefy?' Compo enquired.

'Compo? What...? Oh my goodness! Compo, is that you?' With that, Beefy dropped his end of the torch, the mouse colony's latest acquisition, and rushed to hug his friend.

'Ooooer,' Fred gurgled as he staggered beneath the weight of the torch. Beaky scrambled over to help him put it down, and the two friends danced together with glee.

'Will you lot pack it in? I'm dying here,' Bumble moaned.

'Crumbs, I forgot all about Bumble. Come on, Fred, give us a hand.'

They all ran to Bumble's aid.

'Leave me, boys, I'm done for,' he croaked.

'Bumble? It's barely caught the end of your tail.'

'Really?'

'Yes, really,' Compo said calmly. 'Come on, lads, help me lift this thing.'

Together they lifted the mousetrap hammer just enough for Bumble to pull his tail out.

'Hardly life-threatening,' Beefy observed, having examined it. 'Come on, let's get Mrs Heyhoe to have a look at it.'

'So what's happened to the entrance?'

'The usual, some maintenance guy working upstairs found it and thought he'd put paid to our comings and goings. But don't worry, we've already found a way round it. Follow me.' With that, Beefy dropped through a knothole they'd pushed out of an antique board. Once through it, they scurried up a ramp into the main corridor of the underground mouse colony.

News of the world travellers' return quickly spread, and soon they were surrounded by many of their friends and relations.

There were cries of 'we were worried sick', 'where have you been?' and 'we thought the worst'. One in particular, 'How on earth did three mice go all the way to India and get back in one piece?' struck a nerve with Bumble. Normally the joker, he attempted to quieten everyone down to explain. The grown-ups shushed the excited younger mice and Bumble began.

'I guess we got back because of cricket, friendship and a war a long time ago.'

By the look of the puzzled faces, this explanation would take some clarification. Compo realised that there was one face missing—Willow. He edged away from the group and made his way down the corridor to her workshop. A makeshift curtain hung in the doorway, and he pulled it gently to one side.

Willow was hard at work refurbishing a bat at her workbench. Behind her on the wall she'd fixed a picture of the famous Indian cricketer, Sachin Tendulkar. She'd found it in a Lord's Brochure, and it showed him walking out to bat in the MCC Bicentenary Celebration Match.

'What's with the picture, got a new hero?' Compo asked.

Willow turned and looked at the picture, her back to him.

'I don't know anything about India, but I know Mr Tendulkar, and he's from India. When the boys saw you on the TV in India, it gave me hope that you'd make it home somehow. So the Indian run machine has been my lucky mascot.'

'He seems to have worked.'

Compo had edged closer to her and rested his paw on her shoulder. 'Funny you should call him the 'Run Machine'. I've just met a slightly smaller version. Let me tell you all about him.'

THE END

Beefy

**Glossary of terms**

MCC - Marylebone Cricket Club

Tuk tuk - a three-wheeled motorised vehicle used as a taxi

Godown - A warehouse

Shabash - Great or well played

Bhai - Brother

Acha - Yes

Swagat hai - Welcome (to my home)

Pheta - A traditional turban

Shahenshah - Emperor

Pye-Dog - Urban street dog

Hawker - A seller of merchandise that can be easily transported

Sula Fizz - Indian Champagne equivalent

Theek hai - Okay

Shamiana - An Indian ceremonial tent or shelter

Chinese Cut - When a batsman gets an inside edge which misses the stumps by a fraction

Derring-do - An action displaying heroic courage.

Mahout - A person who works with elephants